"I'm not trying to discourage you."

As desperate as Abigail was, she also couldn't force this man into doing something so difficult. This had to be what Isaac wanted. "If this is so hard for you, surely Dr. Rosen can find you a different internship."

"It's the only internship this summer. I've got to get my degree by the end of the summer so I can take over at Camp Guffey because my mentor is retiring. There's no extension. If I don't have my degree, I don't get the job. And this is what I see my life's work being."

The passion in Isaac's voice, despite the fact that he was still white-knuckle gripping her hand, brought an even deeper understanding of just how difficult this was for Isaac. While it would have been easy to give in and say that he could work without dealing with the horses, for safety's sake, she couldn't have someone this terrified on staff.

They would have to work through it together.

Danica Favorite loves the adventure of living a creative life. She loves to explore the depths of human nature and follow people on the journey to happily-ever-after. Though the journey is often bumpy, those bumps refine imperfect characters as they live the lives God created them for. Oops, that just spoiled the endings of Danica's stories. Then again, getting there is all the fun. Find her at danicafavorite.com.

Books by Danica Favorite

Love Inspired

Shepherd's Creek

Journey to Forgiveness
The Bronc Rider's Twins
A Cowboy for the Summer

Double R Legacy

The Cowboy's Sacrifice
His True Purpose
A True Cowboy
Her Hidden Legacy

Three Sisters Ranch

Her Cowboy Inheritance
The Cowboy's Faith
His Christmas Redemption

Visit the Author Profile page at LoveInspired.com for more titles.

A Cowboy
for the Summer

Danica Favorite

LOVE INSPIRED

INSPIRATIONAL ROMANCE

LOVE INSPIRED®
INSPIRATIONAL ROMANCE

ISBN-13: 978-1-335-58659-9

A Cowboy for the Summer

Copyright © 2023 by Danica Favorite

For questions and comments about the quality of this book, please contact us at CustomerService@Harlequin.com.

Love Inspired
22 Adelaide St. West, 41st Floor
Toronto, Ontario M5H 4E3, Canada
www.LoveInspired.com

Printed in U.S.A.

Be strong and of a good courage, fear not,
nor be afraid of them: for the Lord thy God, he
it is that doth go with thee; he will not fail thee,
nor forsake thee.

—*Deuteronomy* 31:6

For Gloria and Fred, you teach me every day that there are so many adventures to be had in life. I hope I am just as adventurous as you two when I'm in my seventies and eighties. Gloria, thank you for sharing Guffey with me. You are an inspiration to me, and I feel very blessed to get to share that special place with you.

Chapter One

This had to be some kind of joke. Isaac Johnston hopped off his motorcycle and stared at the expansive stable complex. A large structure that seemed too enormous to be called a barn stood before him, surrounded by smaller buildings and arenas. Oh, he knew that uppity Abigail Shepherd had been born with a silver spoon in her mouth, but he hadn't expected this place to be quite so nice. Like something in a movie, only Shepherd's Creek Stables was real. If his original internship with Second Chances Foster Care Camp hadn't been canceled at the last minute due to lack of funding, he'd have gotten right back on his bike and ridden out.

The last thing he needed to get his master's in counseling was an internship, and the only one available would have him stuck babysitting a bunch of rich kids who didn't know what hardship was.

Exactly the opposite of what he aspired to do in his life.

But if this was what he had to do to get through, he'd face it like every other challenge. Do what was necessary, and move on.

Like greeting the smiling woman stepping out of the expansive ranch house that was bigger than anything he'd ever been raised in. Isaac had been in enough foster homes growing up that he had a pretty good idea of what normal people lived in—and it wasn't this.

"Isaac! Hello!" Abigail greeted him warmly, but the fake kind of warm you gave your worst enemy because you were forced to be nice. He was familiar with that greeting as well.

"Nice place you got here," he said slowly, gesturing at the stable compound.

He hated the way the smile lit up her face. She was so pretty when she smiled, which was rarely in his presence. It almost made him like her. Almost.

"Thank you," she said. "We have done so much work on it over the past few years.

It's almost a different place from when my cousin Josie came home a few years ago."

Josie. Right. Josie Shepherd King, emphasis on the *Shepherd*, was the owner of Shepherd's Creek Stables and had created a partnership with one of the recreational departments in the Denver area, allowing them to use these facilities for their summer enrichment programs, along with the local kids. He didn't know all the details, except that Josie was somehow connected to the internship director at the university, and it was by Josie's grace and favor that both he and Abigail had internships here. He didn't think it was fair that Abigail could use a job she already had for internship credit, but she'd gotten it approved. Nepotism at its finest.

One more reason this was not his jam. No one ever handed him anything in life, so he had nothing in common with this spoiled princess he was stuck with for the summer. Worse, his goal was to work with troubled youth, not overindulged brats whose parents could afford to send them to horse camp.

Abigail glanced at his motorcycle, then back at him. "Where's your stuff? Didn't Dr. Rosen explain that you'd be staying here?"

It had been mentioned, but Isaac had ignored it. He wasn't about to stay at some fancy place like this. It wasn't like it was a sleepaway camp and he was a counselor.

"I was planning on commuting."

"It's an hour and a half each way," she said.

Isaac shrugged. "I listen to audiobooks."

She looked at him like she was surprised he was into books. He got that a lot, but Abigail shouldn't have made such an assumption. They were both working on the same master's degree, and were both at the top of their class, which meant he obviously did his share of reading. But he could guarantee that getting this far in his education had been a lot more difficult for him.

"How do you do that on a motorcycle? Doesn't the wind make it hard to hear?"

Oh.

"I have a special headset in my helmet that lets me listen to things. Most people have music, but I like my books."

The smile on her face was almost nauseating. Like she'd plastered it there and it would hurt if she took it off.

"What kind of books do you like?" she asked.

"Nothing you'd be into," he said. Then

he stepped forward. "Look. Can we cut this nice act? I know you can't stand me, and I'm not a fan of yours, either, so let's stop pretending."

Abigail looked like he'd just slapped her. But at least that fake smile was finally gone.

"Fine," she said. "I'm trying to be polite, but you're right. I don't want you here any more than you want to be here, but you need the grade, and the stables need the help. What's it going to take for us to have a professional, cordial working relationship?"

Cordial. One of those highfalutin words that made him wonder if she was at all in touch with reality.

"Why do you have to use such fancy words?" he asked.

Abigail shrugged. "Why not? There are so many great words in the English language, why not use them? I love to read, that's why I was curious what books you like. It would be nice to try to find common ground."

Okay, fine. He was being a bit of a jerk. He'd just been so irritated that Abigail, of all people, represented his only hope at getting his degree in time to take the job he so desperately wanted. Running Camp Guffey, right on Guffey Lake in Minnesota.

His first summer there as a camper, under the guidance of Mr. P, he'd finally seen a glimmer that he wasn't a worthless throwaway and that he could make something of himself.

When he'd aged out of the campership program, he continued going back as a camp counselor, but to be a full-fledged counselor, he had to have a degree. Isaac had worked two, sometimes three, jobs to get through school, but he'd done it. Or at least after this internship.

Mr. P had told him that after this summer, he'd be retiring, and he was looking for someone like Isaac to fill his shoes and run the camp. But without his degree, the hiring committee would not consider him. It didn't matter that Isaac had more experience than anyone besides Mr. P in working at the camp. Isaac had done every job there and could run it inside and out. More than that, Isaac knew what it was like to be one of those kids, how having someone like Mr. P, who understood, made all the difference between making something of yourself and a life on the streets.

The rich people holding the purse strings didn't understand that. All they saw was a piece of paper, and that was the key to your worth.

Which meant he'd play along with Abigail and her idea of finding common ground. It would be good practice for the inevitable hobnobbing he'd have to do with the board of directors who controlled the foundation that kept the camp running.

"I like thrillers," he finally said.

"Me too." Abigail's smile was genuine for a change. "Who's your favorite author?"

Feeling a bit sheepish, he told her, but when he did, her grin widened.

"Me, my cousin Josie, and my sister, Laura, absolutely love her. We trade her books back and forth and are constantly talking about them. You should come to our book club sometime."

She'd had him at a shared love of thrillers, lost him at book club.

"I'm not the book club type," he said. "But thanks anyway."

Abigail laughed. "It's not as stuffy as it sounds. We make yummy snacks, pig out, and talk about the books."

There it was. That annoying, chipper voice that went with her "if you believe you can do it, and you try hard enough" lectures she gave in class that made him want to jump out the window. It was easy for a person who grew up in a place like this to believe that anything was possible. But someone like him, who was one of the rare few to get out of the bad situation he'd grown up in, he knew better.

Maybe he'd be less bitter if it wasn't for the fact that he'd just buried his childhood best friend, Jimmy McAllister. He'd thought Jimmy had finally overcome the drug addiction that had plagued him since they were fourteen. Isaac had even paid for Jimmy's last trip to rehab. Jimmy had been clean for over a year, but one bad breakup, a few missed doses of his meds, and that was all it took. Isaac got the phone call that Jimmy had died of an overdose.

Trying wasn't enough. And Isaac wasn't so naive as to believe he could save them all. But if he could do the same thing for someone that Mr. P had done for him, it was worth it.

Isaac had spent too many class sessions debating Abigail over her silly ideas to think he was ever going to convince her how wrong she was. He'd mastered the art of sucking it up and telling people what they wanted to hear to get a job done. This would be no different.

Fortunately, he was spared from having to be polite about her book club by a man pulling up on an ATV.

"Everything okay?" the man asked as he got off.

"Yes," Abigail said. "Brady, come meet Isaac. He's our new intern."

Before Isaac could step forward to shake the man's hand, another man on an ATV pulled up.

"What's going on?" he asked.

"This is Isaac," Abigail said with that same cheerful voice, like she was absolutely clueless that these guys were checking him out.

"Nice to meet you." The guy got off his ATV and shook Isaac's hand. "I'm Wyatt Nelson."

Wyatt Nelson. That name sounded familiar, and as Isaac took another look at the guy, he thought he knew why.

"As in the world champion bronc rider?" Isaac asked.

A broad grin filled Wyatt's face. "I've worn his boots a time or two. But here, I'm just one of the hands."

Wow. As if Isaac hadn't already felt incredibly out of place here, he was talking to a man who made a healthy six figures a year riding broncs, yet called himself just one of the hands.

Still, this was a connection Isaac could use. "One of the at-risk kids I mentor in Denver is a huge fan. As a reward for accomplishing his goals, I took him to see you ride at the National Western Stock Show. You're a talented rider."

As soon as the words were out of his mouth, Isaac felt stupid for sharing. Guys like Wyatt probably had to deal with crazed fans all the time, and here he was gushing over him.

"It's a real honor to hear that," Wyatt said. "At-risk youth, huh? I don't know what your program allows, but if there's a way to make it happen, I'd love to have him come down here and spend time with the horses. Or, maybe I could go up there and meet him."

Wyatt glanced over at Abigail, then continued. "If it wasn't for this place, and people like Abigail in my life, I'd have gone down a very different road."

"Abigail?" Isaac turned his gaze to the woman standing near them.

He'd expected her to have that same prissy stance he'd gotten to know in class, except as he saw the looks she and Wyatt exchanged, he noticed a softening. A tenderness. Like she was human, after all.

"My folks weren't really the parental type," Wyatt said. "The stables gave me a family I didn't have. Though she was just a girl herself, Abigail mothered us all. Gave up her childhood to make sure we all had one."

Then he looked over at Brady. "I didn't have siblings, but Brady and Cash, God rest his soul, were my brothers. And I am the most blessed man in the world that I can call Abigail's sister, Laura, my wife."

Isaac remembered the news stories about the tragic death of rodeo cowboy Cash Fisher and how close he'd been to Wyatt.

"Anyway," Wyatt continued, "I didn't have a real family, but God saw fit to put people in my life who served that purpose, and if I can do that for someone else, even to inspire them as a role model, that's my way of paying it forward."

It almost seemed like Wyatt and Isaac had more in common than Isaac would have thought.

Though Isaac couldn't have imagined Abigail understanding hardship, the tender expression on her face made him wonder if he hadn't been judging her too harshly.

"We needed you just as much as you needed us," Abigail said softly. "Besides, as you've learned, families are made up of a lot of interesting moving parts. Ultimately, they're what you make them."

Looking back at Isaac, she said, "We're a bit overwhelming and confusing, but you'll get used to it. Anyway, you'll be working closely with Brady and Wyatt, so it's good that you've met them right away."

Something changed in the air as Abigail spoke, and before Isaac could try to make sense of it, a couple of trucks pulled into the parking lot.

"Almost class time," Brady said. "We've got some regular classes happening before camp starts. We need to get ready. We'll have more of a chance to talk at supper, and you can meet the rest of the crew."

The two men hopped on their ATVs and headed back toward the barn.

"Come on," Abigail said. "Let me give you a tour before things start to get busy."

Whatever softness she'd had when Brady and Wyatt were there had disappeared, replaced by the firm woman familiar to Isaac. Even her back and shoulders had straightened, like she was a dutiful soldier.

He'd been certain that getting through this summer was going to be miserable, but it seemed like he'd have an ally in Wyatt. Or at least someone Abigail could thaw around.

Who was Abigail Shepherd? As part of him said he didn't care, another part of him asked if maybe it was worth finding out.

Abigail didn't know why she was so nervous walking Isaac to the barn. Maybe it was because Wyatt had revealed more about her past than she liked to share. Everyone around here just took her past for granted as fact. But the few times she'd revealed it to people who didn't grow up around Shepherd's Creek, they did this whole "poor Abigail, wow, Abigail is so strong," thing that made her seem like more of a martyr than she was.

Yes, it was true that after her mom died, she'd helped raise her sister, Laura, and her cousin Josie. But while outsiders saw it as extraordinary, to Abigail it was just what you did for family. Wyatt said she'd given up her childhood, but what else was she supposed to have done? Sure, she'd have loved to have fallen in love, gotten married, and had children. But for the sake of her family, she'd given up on those dreams. She could content herself with the love of her cousin, sister, and their families. For a woman in her forties, that was the best she could hope for. Sometimes, she did secretly wish for a love like what Laura and Wyatt had, or what Josie and Brady had. But men looked past women her age and focused on those who were younger, prettier, and in better shape. She didn't have anything to offer a man other than her loyalty. So she satisfied herself with a life that was good enough, counting the blessings she did have, and ignored the idea of wanting something more.

Anyway. Back to business. Her personal feelings didn't matter in this situation. Since Josie had just had a baby, rather than finding someone to replace the office lady who'd moved away, they'd moved Josie to the office instead of working with campers so she could have the baby with her. However, to run the camp for the summer, they needed an extra person with experience working with children, and Isaac was the only one who'd applied. He might not be the ideal candidate, but he was all she had. No Isaac, no camp this summer. And they absolutely needed camp this summer to go well so that they were eligible for one of the grants Josie was applying for. If they got the grant, they'd be able to offer more scholarships for families who otherwise wouldn't be able to afford camp. Her dream of growing the summer day-camp program for Shepherd's Creek was on its way to coming true.

She pasted a smile on her face and gestured at the grounds. "This is Shepherd's Creek Stables."

Isaac looked at her like she was an idiot. Which, okay, she was stating the obvious, but being around him always made her so tongue-tied. It was like he was constantly judging her for not following his calling of working with the worst of the worst. But that was what he never seemed to understand. Abigail, too, had a calling, and it was to be here, with her family. They might not be serving the same underprivileged children Isaac always talked about, but so many of the working-class families in their community—as well as the community the rec center served—could barely put food on the table, let alone send their kids to a horse camp. Unfortunately, they didn't meet the income threshold for outside assistance, but that didn't mean they didn't need help, too. Which was why making this summer successful was so important. The stables would be able to extend their ability to help more children attend camp.

As far as Abigail's other hopes, she was mostly living out the life she wanted, and was even achieving a dream she'd never thought possible—that of getting her degree in counseling.

Sure, she'd have loved to have accepted the invitation from one of their former riders to go to her beach wedding in Costa Rica. But a June wedding and summer at the stables didn't mix. They barely had the staff they needed to run the program as it was. She couldn't leave them in the lurch.

Whatever dreams she had besides this degree, well, they weren't as important. Someday things would slow down enough for things like travel. Until then, she could content herself with the idea that she'd already accomplished far more in life than she'd ever hoped for. To ask for more seemed almost greedy.

The stables needed her. She'd been either

running or helping run this place for as long as she could remember, and none of the others in the family had the experience she did. This was the price she paid to help the youth of this community and, more importantly, to keep her family together.

Maybe it wasn't as grand as Isaac's ideas of saving the world, but Abigail was making a difference in her own way.

And all those other secret dreams—those would remain secret.

As she explained the history of the stables and its basic operations, she could see Isaac's eyes glazing over. He'd shown more personality when talking with Wyatt, and part of her wished Wyatt could be the one giving the tour. But Wyatt had his own responsibilities, and like every other unpleasant job Abigail had, she'd simply smile and press on.

As they approached the barn, little Katie Larkins ran over. "Miss Abigail!" Katie gave her a big hug. "I've been practicing the rope trick you taught me."

As Abigail breathed in the little girl's warm scent, peace came over her. This was why she did this. Why she was willing to bring in someone as insufferable as Isaac Johnston to help this summer. At the rate their programs with the rec center were growing, they couldn't handle the influx of kids without adequate staffing, because she was already committed to helping the local kids as well.

She released the little girl and smiled at her. "Well. Show me."

Katie didn't need further encouragement. She set her backpack down and pulled out her rope, busying herself with getting ready for the trick.

As Katie twirled her rope, Abigail's heart swelled with pride. The little girl was picking up the rope tricks easily, and with every new thing Katie learned, she also gained a level of self-confidence. That was the other thing Abigail couldn't quantify to people like Isaac. How does one measure the emotional growth of children?

"That's amazing," Abigail said. "You just barely started the trick last week, and you're already doing it like a pro."

The smile on Katie's face made it easier to forget the way Isaac had been scowling at Abigail. Almost. The trouble with Isaac's scowls was that he was so good-looking, even the angry glances he gave her made her heart skip a beat. That was the pathetic thing about this all. The man who pushed all of her buttons was also incredibly easy to look at. Thankfully, he was nearly twenty years her junior, so any of this weird attraction she felt toward him meant nothing. It wasn't like they had a chance at a real future or real relationship, even if they could find a way to get along. No, Abigail could simply admire the eye candy and let the rest go.

A man as young and handsome as Isaac would never be interested in her.

When Katie finished the trick, Isaac said to her, "That was pretty neat. I've never seen anything like it. Do you think you could show me how?"

The way Katie's face lit up made Abigail melt just a little bit. How could he be so absolutely infuriating and yet so sweet?

"Well," Katie said, "I'm only a beginner, but if you really want to learn, Abigail is the expert. She's been on TV and everything."

Abigail gave a small laugh. "It was just a promotional video we do for the stables. It's no big deal."

"I've never been on TV," Katie said, her eyes wide with hero worship.

"Well maybe someday." To take the heat off of her, she gestured at Isaac. "This is

Isaac. He is going to be one of our camp counselors this summer. Why don't you help him learn something? I'm sure you can teach him a basic loop. And what have I told you about the basics?"

Katie beamed. "The basics are the foundation to anything you do in life. Always master the basics because they'll take you far."

So many of the kids wanted to start out with all the complicated things they'd seen other people do, whether it be trick roping, riding, or really any other facet of life. Abigail had found that by teaching the children this principle, she got a lot less complaining about not being able to do more complicated things before the children were ready.

Katie reached into her bag and handed Isaac one of her extra ropes. "Here. Take this. Now I'm going to slowly walk you through how to make a loop, so pay attention. But if you run into trouble, you just let me know and I'll help you."

She didn't know which she found more tender and sweet, the sight of the little girl teaching this big burly man how to twirl a rope, or the fact that he was so tender in allowing her to do so. Nothing about Isaac said he would be open to the Western way of life. It was one of the reasons why she'd been hesitant about having him come here, even though they hadn't had any other options. Sure, some cowboys did ride motorcycles, but Isaac had shown up decked out in leathers with a tough-guy attitude that seemed completely out of place here. But all of that melted away with his simple interaction with the little girl.

In class, Abigail and Isaac had always found a million things to disagree on. She'd hoped that when they'd landed on loving the same books that they might have found something in common, but it had only seemed to make Isaac even angrier toward her. But this, encouraging a small child, might be the exact common ground they needed. After all, they didn't have to become besties to work with kids. All they really needed was to be on the same team when it came to the kids, and clearly they were.

Maybe having Isaac around wouldn't be so bad after all. And, when he got annoying with his insufferable opinions that drove her nuts, she would keep scenes like this in mind. A man who was willing to give this kind of attention to a child had to have something good inside him.

Chapter Two

By the time Katie finished teaching Isaac how to twirl a rope, Isaac felt pretty good about his abilities in the rope department. More than that, he was feeling a lot better about having to work with Abigail. Just like when she was talking with Brady and Wyatt, her stuck-up attitude had softened, and she seemed almost like a different person. Maybe that was the key to working with her. Finding areas where she was comfortable and letting her loose.

She seemed confident enough in the classes they'd taken together, but she always had this no-nonsense, "I'm better than you" attitude. Here, though, she'd gotten down to the level of a child, and, even though she was clearly an expert with ropes, she had deferred to that same child, allowing her to take the lead.

Not many people did that, and it took a special person to let a child be in control.

"You're going to be late for your riding class if you don't hurry," Abigail told Katie, a gentle smile on her face.

Katie stuffed the ropes back in her bag. "Uh oh. I'd better get going. Brady makes us do push-ups when we're late."

As the little girl ran off, Isaac grinned at Abigail, who'd started walking toward the barn. "Push-ups, huh? He seems pretty hardcore."

Abigail laughed, like she realized he was joking with her. That was the other problem between the two of them. Half the time in class, when Isaac would crack a joke, Abigail would take him seriously, like he was trying to insult her, when it hadn't been his intention at all.

"What they don't know is that even though it's technically a punishment, we are helping them develop their upper-body strength so that they can do all of the things like roping and riding even better. But Brady always makes it fun, so despite my calling it a punishment, it's not."

He heard the hesitation in her voice, the same insecurity as when he tried to joke with her.

"Hey, I wasn't criticizing," he said. "I think it's great that they have consequences for being late, and it's absolutely brilliant that the consequences actually help them get better. So many people don't tie consequences to actions or make them relevant to what's really going on."

Even though he hated fake smiles, Isaac did his best to smile at her, to show her they were on the same team. But as her face softened, he realized that his smile wasn't as fake as he thought it would be. He genuinely liked seeing this side of Abigail, and if a simple smile was all it took, he supposed he didn't have to fake it.

Isaac had often been told that his ordinary resting face looked hostile, so maybe some of the communication issues weren't entirely her fault.

"I know it's not exactly the same, but one of the foster homes I was in for a while was really into motocross. They signed me up for some lessons, and when we were late, we would have to sit out part of the ride. I always thought that was a terrible way to punish someone for tardiness because the whole reason you don't want to be tardy to learn something like riding a motorcycle is that you need to be there for every bit of the lesson for safety reasons. Time not spent on a motorcycle is time not spent learning how to be safe."

The smile Abigail gave him made him realize that he'd been right to pay attention to her reactions, and rather than feeding off of the negativity that he perceived, they simply had to communicate about it.

Funny how they'd been in classes together all this time and he hadn't realized that until now.

"That's exactly why we don't punish students by taking away their ride time. They need every opportunity they can get to practice, for the exact same reason you mentioned about motorcycles. A horse is just as dangerous as a motorcycle, and every minute spent with one is another way to become safer in your interactions."

Isaac chuckled. "I suppose you're right. But I'll admit that I'm very thankful that my job here is to work with the kids, not the horses."

Abigail stopped walking and stared at him

for second. "What do you mean? This is a horse camp."

"Yes, but I'm here for an internship to work with the kids."

"Who are learning to ride horses," Abigail said, enunciating every word.

Well, this was awkward. No sooner did the only internship he'd been able to get begin than it was over.

"Surely there are other things I can do with the kids that don't involve horses," he said.

Abigail stared at him. "To a degree," she said. "But the primary activity here is all about the horses. I thought that was clear in the internship description."

Isaac took a deep breath. "There were many other things listed in the description that had nothing to do with horses."

The expression on Abigail's face was similar to the ones he'd seen in class that he couldn't stand. "So what exactly is your problem with horses?" she asked.

It probably wouldn't be a point in his favor if he told her just how much he couldn't stand horses, so instead, he said, "I don't have a lot of experience with them, or any other animal, for that matter."

Though he braced himself for a stiff response, he was met with a warm smile. "That's okay," she said. "We can easily teach you anything you need to know."

Though he sensed the same kind attitude she'd had when asking Katie to teach him to rope, this was not the same thing.

"I really would prefer not to be around the horses," he said.

She gave him a funny look. "Are you allergic?"

It would be easy to lie and say yes, but that wasn't his style. And with the way she looked at him, it was obvious she wasn't going to simply let it go.

"I had bad experiences with horses when I was a kid," he said.

Instead of looking sympathetic, Abigail didn't seem bothered by his confession. "We can work with that. In fact, this will be perfect for you because one of the reasons we like exposing kids to horses who have never been around them is so that they won't be afraid. I've met a lot of kids who had bad experiences with horses, and even though you're an adult, I'm confident that I can help you, too."

Yeah, that wasn't what he was going for here.

"I think it's great that you can help kids,"

he said. "But trust me when I say that horses are really not my thing."

"So what happened with you and horses?" she asked.

He should have known that the stubborn woman who argued with him over everything in class was going to keep fighting him on this issue.

He wanted to tell her that it was none of her business, but even he had to admit that if he was going to have to be around horses, he should probably explain his history. And, maybe if she understood how bad his experience was, she'd give him a pass and let him do this his way.

"Growing up in the foster care system, I had a lot of foster families. Many of them tried to do different activities with us, thinking it would give us good life experiences. However, this was not the case with horses. One of the families took us to a petting zoo, where we got to feed the animals. I hadn't even gotten to the point where I was feeding the horse, and the horse reached through the fence and bit my arm."

Even though there wasn't a scar from the incident, Isaac rubbed the place where he'd been bit, remembering it just as it happened.

"The employee at the petting zoo said the horse had never done anything like that before, and someone suggested that he thought the fruit on my shirt was something to eat—I don't know. I just know that I was standing there, minding my own business, and the horse bit me."

He expected her to laugh, like others had when he'd told that story, but she nodded sympathetically. "That must've been very scary for you. How old were you?"

Oh, yes. The therapist voice. He knew exactly what she was doing here, since they both were in the same class that trained them to do so. Though part of him wanted to resist her efforts, he also knew that his resistance was telling. This, too, was part of therapy, part of what needed to happen for him to heal. Until now, he hadn't thought that this particular issue was necessary to resolve, but here they were, at a horse camp, so clearly it was time.

"I was seven," he said. "I cried so hard, and I remember my foster mother shushing me, telling me not to make a scene, and my foster brother calling me a big baby."

Abigail gestured at a nearby bench. "That must've been really hard to have such a scary situation and have your emotions dismissed like that. Why don't we go sit, and you can tell me some more?"

Okay, fine. She got him. He always thought that she'd be a terrible counselor because she thought she was so much better than everyone else and was so strong in her opinions. And yet here she was, so easily able to get to the heart of his pain and offer him compassion.

He still didn't necessarily want to talk about his issues with horses, nor did he have any desire to have anything to do with the creatures he saw being ridden in the distance. But honestly, if he was going to be forced to work with this issue, something about sharing it with Abigail made him feel safe.

Once they were seated on the bench, he said, "It was pretty awful. I think that's one of the reasons I decided to work with kids like me. I was shuttled from foster home to foster home, and no one ever validated my feelings. That's what so many kids need. They just need to know that it's okay to feel the way they do."

Abigail nodded, an understanding look on her face. "I completely agree. Though

I know my uncle Joe did the best he could in raising us, he saw any sign of emotion as weakness, and we would get in trouble for showing them. For some reason, I intuitively knew that it wasn't good to do so, and I always worked hard to help my sister and cousin deal with theirs. But I was just a kid, so of course I made my mistakes. That's one of the reasons I wanted to get a degree in counseling, so I could do better. It's clear you're similarly motivated."

Hearing her story and seeing the compassion on her face made him realize once again that they had more in common than he thought. "I didn't think you'd get it," he admitted.

"More than most people know," she said. "We're all taught to deal with difficult emotions in different ways, and it's not surprising that something so terrifying for a child met with such a lack of compassion would turn into a lifelong fear of horses. But I'd love to create a safe space here for you to work through it. It's very unusual for a horse to bite unprovoked, though some horses are biters. Would you be willing to work with me to get past that fear?"

Well, she was good. Before today, he would

have said he had no reason to move past that fear, but now he realized that this was bigger than horses. This was about the little boy who felt invalidated so many times in his life. Except, there were still more horse issues at hand.

"I wish that was the only bad experience I had with a horse," he said. "A couple years later, a different set of foster parents took me to a horseback riding place, and the horse kicked me so hard that I had a painful bruise for weeks."

Once again, Abigail nodded slowly. "How did your foster parents react?"

He stared at her for a moment. Most people asked him what he had done wrong; he hadn't done anything. But no, Abigail wanted to know about the emotional support he'd received.

"My foster mother was very upset. After yelling at the stable people, she whisked me away to the ER, where they made sure that I wasn't seriously injured, but for weeks afterward, she went on and on about this terrible place that would let a precious little boy get injured. She told me the horses were too dangerous, and she would never subject me to that again."

As he told the story from an emotional perspective, he could see how his foster mother's reaction was just as damaging as the previous foster family's.

"That must've also been scary," Abigail said.

"Yes," Isaac agreed. "And then, another family took me to a dude ranch for a week, and the first day there, we went for a trail ride. They knew I was afraid of horses, so they gave me the gentlest horse in the bunch. I got on that thing and kicked it, and it wouldn't go. Once we got moving though, it was kinda neat. I started to relax. But on the way home, the horse just took off on me. I did all the things they told me to stop my horse, and it just ran and ran. At one point, it bucked a little, and I fell off, breaking my arm."

He watched her face as he told the story, noticing how she was engaged in what he had to say, not trying, like others did, to diminish what he'd experienced or make excuses for the horse.

"Ouch," she said. "What a terrible way to start a vacation."

Isaac nodded. "It was the worst vacation of my life. My foster parents complained about how much money they'd spent only to have it ruined. The funny thing is, they continued to enjoy the rest of the week at the dude ranch after we'd gone and gotten a cast on my arm. I was stuck in our room reading the whole time."

He chuckled at the memory. "Actually, it wasn't that bad. I liked having an excuse to do nothing but read, even though it was hard with a cast on my arm."

Abigail laughed with him, and he couldn't help thinking how much he loved the sound of it. For someone so annoying, she wasn't half bad. Actually, even though she was a bit older than him, he had to admit that she was kind of pretty. Okay, not kind of. She was definitely pretty. So weird to think about that when he just spilled his guts to her about what he could see was an irrational fear. But calling it irrational didn't make it any less fearful.

"A week stuck in a cabin with a bunch of books sounds wonderful," Abigail said. "But I can see how all those things put together would make it so you didn't like horses."

Though he knew she was trained to affirm him, hearing those affirmations made it seem almost okay that he was afraid of horses.

"So you get it then? You'll figure out a way for me to not have to deal with them, right?"

Abigail laughed slightly, then shook her head. "Oh no. You don't get off that easily. I agree that what happened was traumatic, and the adults around you didn't support you in a positive manner. But I also know that it's not serving you to avoid horses because of your past. Think about every painful thing we've ever been through. If we avoided everything that caused pain in the past, we'd all live in bubbles."

Abigail stood and held out her hand. "Let me help you. Not just because having you terrified of horses at a horse stable is a liability, but because you don't deserve to live with that fear anymore. I promise I will do everything I can to keep you safe, and no matter what happens, I'm here to support you."

He'd spent the past couple years thinking of her as his biggest nemesis in class. But here she was, offering him a level of compassion and kindness he hadn't expected. Though part of him would argue that the only reason he was agreeing to this was so he could graduate in time to take the job at Camp Guffey, the rest of him was eager to finally find freedom.

Isaac stood and took her hand. "Okay," he said.

Unbelievable. Abigail would have never thought to connect with the most irritating guy in all of her classes in such a deep way. He'd opened up to her so unexpectedly and so beautifully that she just wanted to hug him, but she was afraid that would cross the line. She was supporting him in a professional capacity, and she had to remember that. They were just colleagues, and she was merely helping him through a rough spot so they could both do their jobs.

But as she held his hand and walked him into the barn, this felt more sacred than just helping a colleague or even a patient, this felt deep and real.

"If it's okay with you, I'd like to introduce you to some of the horses. We're going to walk straight through the barn and past some of them in their stalls. The stall doors are always kept locked, and we have strict rules about entering and leaving the stalls, so as long as everybody is in their stall, you're perfectly safe."

She could feel his tension grow in the hand she still held, and she gave it a squeeze. "I know others have told you that you're safe around horses, and the truth is that because horses have brains, they'll never be one hundred percent safe. But I promise you, as long as you are here at the stables, I will do everything I can to make sure you are safe. If at any moment you don't feel that way, just tell me, and we'll make it better."

He relaxed slightly, then gave a nervous laugh. "It's funny, everyone thinks I'm crazy because they see motorcycles as being unsafe. But as you pointed out, horses have brains, and motorcycles don't. I'm the brains behind the motorcycle, and I trust myself. Having to rely on a creature with a mind of its own that can't fully communicate with you, that's terrifying."

Once again, Abigail squeezed his hand. "I've never been on a motorcycle, and I'll admit I've always thought them a little too dangerous. Especially with the way people zoom past here above the speed limit. I get what you're saying about you being the brain behind the motorcycle, but the trouble is all the other drivers whose brains you don't know."

Isaac laughed, no longer sounding nervous. "I'll give you that," he said. "There are a lot of scary drivers out on the road."

Sharing a moment of laughter was exactly what they had both needed, and Abigail led him to the stall where they kept her personal horse.

"This is my buddy, Simba. I like to call him Simbasaurus rex because, like the Tyrannosaurus rex memes show, as scary as his appearance is sometimes, he is really just a silly old goofball."

She smiled at Isaac, who once again looked slightly fearful. "It's okay if you're scared. But Simba is the gentlest horse you'll ever meet, and I've met hundreds. However, I would be really honored if you would trust me to help you pet him so you can see for yourself."

Abigail had dealt with many people afraid of horses over the years, and she knew that part of helping them get over the fear was a lot of positive experiences over and over to show them that just because you had one—or in Isaac's case, three—bad experience with a horse, it didn't mean they all had to be.

For a moment, he looked like he wanted to run. But as the expressions flitted across his face, she could see him steeling himself to do the hard thing. Abigail's heart filled with the same pride she had in her students as they, too, faced things that they were scared of, whether it be loping for the first time or trying a new trick that was difficult. That was really what Abigail's work and life were about. Helping others face their fears and overcome. She just had a pretty cool way of doing it by using horses.

"I've never been so terrified in my life," Isaac admitted. "And that's saying something, because as a teen, I was one of the top-ranked motocross riders in my division. Some of the pictures of me doing backflips are amazing, but they are one of the most dangerous things you can do."

She would have never imagined the big strong man in her classes being so scared of anything.

"I'm right here with you," she said.

Abigail opened the stall door and led him inside. "Until I know that you're comfortable with horses and feel safe in doing so, I never want you to go into a horse's stall without me or someone like Wyatt or Brady. Ordinarily, I would protect your privacy, but I am going to tell them about your fears. It's important for them to know so they can also keep you safe."

For a moment, Isaac tensed, and Abigail could understand his hesitation. No one likes to admit to their insecurities, especially someone like Isaac, who always seemed to want to get the last word in.

"They seem like good enough guys, I suppose." Doubt filled his eyes, but his chest rose and fell like he was taking a deep breath. "I know I have to trust the team I'm working for. So I guess that's okay."

His vulnerability softened Abigail toward him even more. He'd been through so much trauma, and yet, he was willing to face it. It was a rare person who was brave enough to go through something like this. She hadn't expected that of him.

"I'm not trying to discourage you or anything," she said. "If this is so hard for you, surely Dr. Rosen can find you a different internship."

As desperate as she was, she also couldn't force this man into doing something so difficult. This had to be what Isaac wanted.

"It's the only internship this summer. I've

got to get my degree by the end of summer so I can take over at Camp Guffey because my mentor is retiring. There's no extension. If I don't have my degree, I don't get the job. And this is what I see my life's work being."

The passion in his voice, despite the fact that he was still white-knuckle gripping her hand, brought an even deeper understanding of just how difficult this was for Isaac. While it would have been easy to give in and say that he could work without dealing with the horses, she couldn't have someone this terrified on staff, for safety's sake.

They would have to work through it together.

But at least now, Abigail had an idea of how they would do that.

She gestured inside the stall. "Why don't we get started then?"

He squeezed her hand tighter, but he took a step forward. At this rate, she was going to end up with a broken hand.

Once they got inside the stall, Abigail said, "Hey, Simbasaur. How's my little man?"

"Little man?" Isaac asked. "He is a giant horse."

Abigail grinned. "Actually he's a little on

the small and scrawny side. But don't tell him that. Everyone makes fun of him for being such a little horse, but I think he's the darlingest boy, and I know it hurts his feelings when people make fun of him."

"He has feelings?"

Simba had started walking over toward them, and Abigail held out her free hand. "Come say hi to Mama and her new friend."

Then Abigail glanced at Isaac. "Of course he has feelings. I think that horses, like many animals, pick up on the emotions of people around them. They know when you love them, they know when you're scared, so they act accordingly. But I'm here, and Simba knows I love him with all my heart."

As if to agree with her, Simba gave a little nicker, stepping into her space and allowing her to pet him.

"There's my good boy."

"You talk to him like he's a person, too," Isaac said.

Abigail stroked Simba's neck softly with her free hand. "Sometimes I feel like he is. But also, when you talk to a horse, they get used to your voice and learn to trust you. Most of the time, they just need to know we don't mean them any harm."

Isaac relaxed slightly, so maybe her words were getting through to him. Or at least he was beginning to understand that he didn't have to be afraid.

"Why is Camp Guffey so special to you?" Abigail said. "I'd like to get you in a different emotional state so Simba can sense something other than fear from you. When he picks up that emotion, he wonders what you're afraid of, so it puts him on alert. If something is scary to you, it must be something for him to worry about."

"I never thought of it that way," he said.

Abigail smiled at Isaac, then turned her attention back to the horse. Though Simba was calm, she wanted to make sure that he was in the best state of mind when Isaac finally decided to take the plunge and bond with the horse.

"He can't communicate with words, so he picks up cues in other ways, like reading our body language and hearing our voices and getting a sense of the energy we put off."

She could feel Isaac relaxing even more as his grip loosened on her hand. "So you talking in a gentle, calm voice helps him relax around nervous me?" Isaac said.

"Exactly. He knows he can trust me. Even

though there's someone here who is scared, he knows I'll keep him safe."

As if to further reassure Simba, she gave him a scratch in his favorite spot. The poor guy was going to get spoiled with all this attention, but if it helped Isaac, it was worth it.

"The thought of horses needing humans to keep them safe seems silly to me," Isaac said. "But you know, it makes sense. Horses, like humans, get abused. I guess in some ways, that makes us a bit of the same, doesn't it?"

The vulnerability in Isaac's voice made Abigail's heart ache. He wasn't just talking from a clinical standpoint, but from personal experience. From the bits of his story she had heard, she could piece together rather easily what his past must have been like. Suddenly, all the fighting they'd done didn't seem to matter so much. The more time she spent with Isaac in this setting, the more she understood just how human he was.

"Absolutely," Abigail said. "Safety is relative. It's easy to feel safe around a creature that treats us right, but when we have reason to mistrust, it's a lot harder."

She turned her attention to Isaac again,

giving him a gentle smile. "I know we don't get along, so it's harder for you to feel safe with me. But I hope you know that with horses, I will do all I can to keep you safe."

Her gaze was met with genuine understanding and compassion, and dare she say it, a smile.

"I know that," he said. "I'm starting to think we've both been misjudging each other. I'm beginning to see you in a new light."

"Me too," she admitted.

For a moment, their eyes locked, and while she wasn't going to add Isaac to her list of besties anytime soon, hopefully, by the end of the summer, she'd at least be able to call him a friend. As it was now, she was gaining a deeper understanding of the man she'd once called an enemy.

"Anyway," he finally said. "About Guffey. It was a camp for foster kids. I went every summer since I was about ten. Up to that point, I'd been bouncing between foster homes. I never felt like I could be the kid they wanted me to be. But at Camp Guffey, I could be me and everyone accepted that."

As Abigail hoped, his posture softened even more, and his breathing became slow and regular.

Isaac grinned. "Mr. P, who became my mentor and whose job I'm taking over at the end of the summer, taught me so much about my value as a person. I think I would've ended up on the streets if it weren't for him."

"That's so great," Abigail said, touched that he'd shared so much with her. Even though they were still holding hands, she didn't feel like he was clinging to her so strongly. Mr. P must've been a powerful force in his life to make him feel so brave and safe.

"Do you want to try to pet Simba now?" she asked.

She looked at Isaac's face, trying to read his expression, but even though he'd softened to her, she still couldn't tell what he was thinking or feeling. Isaac nodded slowly.

"Mr. P is the one who taught me to try everything, even if it scared me. Granted, he was talking about eating my spinach and using the giant rope swing to swing into the lake, but I think it applies here."

Abigail laughed, and Simba, good boy that he was, simply stood there. Horses were skittish, and some would react to laughter, but Simba was pretty bombproof. That was one of the reasons she'd chosen him for this experiment.

"Well then, let's do this for Mr. P," Abigail said, putting a little more enthusiasm in her voice than she ordinarily would, but wanting to make everyone feel as comfortable as possible.

Isaac nodded, and Abigail guided his hand to the horse. At first, she kept hers with his, but the more confident his strokes got the more she backed off to let him do it on his own.

"He's so soft," Isaac said.

"I try to groom him every day, even if I don't ride him. It's our special time together, and it's so good for us to make sure we're constantly connecting and bonding."

Isaac glanced over at her. "It's your therapy, isn't it?"

Abigail smiled. No one had ever put it that way, and it felt weird to open up to someone she'd never gotten along with like this. But Isaac had opened up to her in so many ways that she wouldn't have thought possible, so it only seemed fair to do the same with him. "Yes. This guy knows all my secrets. When I've had a bad day, a little time with him goes a long way in making me feel better. I tell Simba everything, and he's always been there for me."

Isaac began stroking the horse on his own, in different places than where she'd shown him. He was feeling more confident now, exploring.

"I briefly had a dog when I was a kid. I used to tell him things, too." The wistful tone in his voice made her smile, though it was a sad story. She wanted to ask him more about the dog, but she'd already pushed pretty hard on him, and he was off in some faraway place, probably remembering. But whatever it was, it made him seem even more peaceful, more willing to bond with the horse.

"You *are* a good boy, aren't you?" he said to Simba, scratching him exactly the way Abigail had.

Simba rewarded him with a gentle nudge of his head, a gesture Abigail loved, and it especially warmed her heart to see that he was doing it to Isaac, and Isaac was accepting it.

"That's Simba's way of saying you are scratching exactly the right spot, and I love it. Please keep it up."

Isaac stepped in closer to Simba, continuing to scratch him and love on him. "He's kind of like a big dog, isn't he?"

Abigail laughed. "Most definitely. Sometimes we joke around and refer to the horses as our big dogs. I'm pretty sure that if he wasn't about six hundred pounds, he'd be a lapdog."

The carefree laugh that came from Isaac warmed Abigail's heart even more. Here was this man, who only a short time ago was absolutely terrified of horses, now able to pet one and joke around. This was an absolute gift.

The past couple of years, Abigail had been praying that God would take Isaac from her life. Nothing mean, but some kind of blessing, like he would get offered a place at another school. All she wanted was for him to be transported far, far away. But God hadn't given her the answer she wanted. Instead, God was showing her how He needed to use her in Isaac's life. Maybe it wasn't some earth-shattering thing, but even something as small as helping him overcome his fear of horses would be doing good.

Abigail took a deep breath, closed her eyes briefly and said a prayer, thanking God for not answering her previous prayers to remove Isaac from her life. She could see now how God's hand had been on this all along, and as she stood beside Isaac, continuing to guide him as he accepted her horse's love, she couldn't wait to see how God would work in their lives for the rest of the summer.

Chapter Three

Isaac would have never believed that he could bond so strongly with a horse. To be honest, if someone had told him he'd pet a horse, he'd have said no way. Yet here he was.

The sound of Wyatt outside the stall snapped him out of his special moment with Simba.

"Chow time," Wyatt said, holding up some hay.

"I'll take it," Abigail said.

She reached over the opening and took the hay from Wyatt, then set it in a feeder on the other side of the stall.

As Simba noticed the food coming in, he turned his attention away from Isaac.

"Sorry, food is always the most important thing to Simba," Abigail said, grinning at him. "But this is also an important lesson in horsemanship. Never get between a horse and his food."

Isaac laughed. "I'm pretty sure that's true of me, too."

"And me," Wyatt said, laughing along with him. "I see Abigail's introducing you to the animals. Make sure she brings you around to everyone, not just her baby."

Abigail glanced at Isaac, as if she was asking for permission, and even though he'd already agreed to share his secret with everyone, it was nice to know she still wanted to make sure it was okay. He gave a small nod in response.

"So, that's going to be the challenging part of the summer," Abigail said. "Isaac has had some bad experiences with horses, and this was me helping him feel not so skittish around them."

He waited for Wyatt to make fun of him the way others had in the past, but Wyatt was thoughtful for a moment, then said, "Abigail is the best at helping people get past their fear of horses. We've had some young kids absolutely in hysterics because they were so terrified, and after working with

Abigail a little bit, they've all gone out riding like champions."

Then he gave a small chuckle. "Not that I'm expecting you to go out on the broncs with me, but you're in good hands."

Isaac's throat tightened at the support from Wyatt and, even more so, Abigail. Sure, he had his share of encouragement through the years, but other than Mr. P and his advisor in the counseling program, he hadn't seen this depth of caring from others.

What he hadn't realized was the way she took the time to get to know people on a deeper level. He supposed it was hard to do with case studies, since you didn't have actual people to interact with and see their hearts. The one group project they'd worked on together had been a disaster because Abigail had simply wanted to get it done, saying she had more important things to do.

But now, he got it. To her, an assignment was just a grade, but when it came to doing the work, she invested more time in the people themselves than he'd ever encountered.

As they exited the stall area, Wyatt followed. "Originally, I'd planned on having you help me with my group because I tend to get a lot of the rough-and-tumble boys, and another pair of hands is always useful. But the last thing I need is someone skittish around horses. Combine boys who like to do dumb stuff and horses, and someone's bound to get hurt."

Though Isaac felt like he made friends with Simba, he couldn't see himself doing the job Wyatt was talking about. Having once been a rowdy boy himself, Isaac wasn't confident enough to handle that and a horse.

"Isaac can work with me," Abigail said quickly. "I get a lot of the special cases, so we tend to go more slowly anyway."

Wyatt laughed. "I see what you did there. If you take Isaac, that means I get Kayla."

As Abigail laughed with him, she turned to Isaac. "Kayla is my cousin Josie's step-daughter, Brady's daughter. I love the girl to death, and she is a huge help with the camps, but she would much rather be out doing dangerous stuff than wrangling little kids. Don't get me wrong, she loves children and is hoping to become a pediatrician someday, but whenever she helps me, I catch her looking longingly at the people in other groups."

It was strange, seeing how they all worked together as a family. Isaac had written it all off as nepotism, but this interaction, plus the greeting he'd received earlier, made him realize that they all saw each other as a team. It wasn't like anyone was being handed anything.

"That kid is an adrenaline lover," Wyatt said, still laughing. "Sometimes I worry about my boys learning from her, but she has such a good heart that I can only hope they turn out half as good as she has."

Isaac marveled at the familial closeness as Wyatt walked away. He'd been in and out of foster homes because his father was abusive and his mother, while she was incredibly loving to Isaac, took drugs as a way to cope, at least until she'd died. So he hadn't had a great example of love from his biological family. He was sure the foster families all tried, but he'd never bonded with any of them the way the people here did with each other. This family was the perfect example of the kind of family he'd always hoped to have for himself.

But that had been just wishful thinking. His father had been incredibly cruel, and in one of his rages, he'd told Isaac that he was going to grow up to be just like him. Worse, his excuse for the abuse was that it was just how children were supposed to be raised. Spare the rod and spoil the child, and all that. He'd been treated the same way his own father had been treated. Even though Isaac had been through a great deal of therapy over the years, he wondered if it would be enough to correct all the damage his father had done. The generational patterns instilled in him were a family legacy he was determined to stop.

Classes must've ended, because Katie, the little girl who taught him how to rope, came running up to them.

"Abigail, guess what?"

The little girl wrapped her arms around Abigail's legs, and Abigail bent to give her a hug. It was strange for Isaac to see all the hugging that went on around this place because in so much of his work with abused children, physical touch had to be done in a careful and regulated way to avoid inadvertently triggering one of the children. Here, though, it seemed like everywhere he looked kids were hugging one another and adults also had open arms.

"Tell me," Abigail said, releasing the little girl from her hug.

"I got to call the drill today," Katie said, then launched into a rapid-fire explanation of everything that happened. Isaac didn't understand most of it, but the way Abigail was smiling, it had to be a good thing.

"Sounds like a great thing," Isaac said, trying to give the little girl encouragement.

Abigail laughed. "That's very sweet, but I can tell from your expression you have no idea what she was talking about. Katie, remember, we have someone new here, and he doesn't know all of our things yet. Can you explain to him what calling the drill means?"

Just as she'd done when asked to teach him a rope trick, Katie straightened like she was suddenly being given a very important duty. Isaac appreciated how much ownership Abigail gave the child, letting her feel important and like she had a role with the adults.

"All of our horses ride in a pattern, which is what we call a drill. With so many horses in the arena at once, everybody has to know where they're supposed to be going. Otherwise, you crash into each other. So…" Katie paused like she was about to deliver big important news "…somebody has to be the leader to tell everyone where they should be so nobody gets hurt. That's what we say is calling the drill. I got to do that today because I got a perfect score on my riding test from last week."

Even though Isaac barely knew the little girl, his heart swelled with the same amount of pride Katie was exuding. "That's awesome. So you have two reasons to celebrate. A perfect score and getting to call the drill. A rock star."

Moments like this, Isaac could hardly understand why anyone would ever abuse a child. He knew that not all kids were as vivacious and giving as Katie, but he had to believe that they all had that same potential. That was the potential he wanted to develop in kids at Camp Guffey. He'd been one of the kids who was hard to love, and he wanted those children to see that they were worthy as well.

A car pulled up, and a woman got out, looking irritated. He didn't need to get a good look at her to know she'd had a really bad day.

"Great," Katie said. "Dad sent the bear to get me."

Abigail looked at the woman then back down at Katie. "Remember what we talked about? Susan is your stepmother, and you need to treat her with respect."

The dejected look on Katie's face tore at Isaac's heart. It was funny how he'd made assumptions about all the people here, and so far, everything was wrong. He'd imagined that a happy little girl like Katie came from a wonderful family, full of love, but as he saw the tense way her stepmother greeted her and Katie's irritable response, he was reminded that things are seldom what they appear to be on the surface.

As Katie shuffled off behind Susan, she looked back at them. "Bye, Abigail. I'll see you next time. Isaac it was nice meeting you, and you remember to practice those rope tricks I taught you."

Isaac grinned, glad to see some of the vivacious little girl back.

He glanced at Abigail, who had her eyes closed. Then they quickly flew open, and she gestured toward another part of the building.

"I guess we should continue with the tour then."

Since no one else seemed to be around, Isaac said, "So what's the story with her and the stepmother?"

Abigail shrugged. "Her parents are divorced and both work long hours to make ends meet. Susan thinks it's a terrible imposition for Katie to be involved in horse activities, and she doesn't get along with Katie much anyway. I think this is the one bright spot in that little girl's life, so I do everything I can to encourage her."

Abigail led him down a covered walkway into another part of the building. "This is where we have our classrooms as well as a few other necessary spaces."

"Do you think she's abused?" Isaac asked.

For a moment, Abigail didn't speak as she fumbled with the set of keys attached to her belt. "I haven't seen any evidence of it, but everyone here is trained to look for abuse, and we're all mandatory reporters. Growing up, things here weren't that easy. While none of us were physically abused, we also didn't have an emotionally healthy upbringing, and now that the stables are being run by a new generation, we decided to do things differently."

Though her words were simple and no-nonsense, they gave him a much deeper look into Abigail's psyche. All this time, he thought she'd lived a perfect life. It was the impression she gave when she talked about her life here at the stables, but different things others had said since he'd been here, combined with this minor revelation, made him realize just how deeply he'd been misjudging her all along.

In a way, Isaac and Abigail were the same.

"That's why you're getting your degree, isn't it?" he asked. "You've always said in class that it was to help you run your family's stables programs, but it's because you want to right the wrongs of the past."

Abigail smiled at him softly. "Partially. I mean yes, I do want the training to make sure that I am doing right by the children who walk through the stables. Even when Uncle Joe was alive, I was reading books about child development and learning so I could do the very best job I could. But also, I just love learning. I spent my whole life wishing I could go to college, but Uncle Joe always laughed at me and said it wasn't necessary. He disowned Josie when she went to college. I wasn't willing to rock the boat or leave these kids behind, so I did what I could on my own. But thanks to my cousin and sister, I started taking classes, and now here I am, almost with my master's. It sounds silly, but this is my ultimate dream come true."

He had heard her talking about how getting her degree was a dream, and he'd thought it was silly that someone would aspire to have a piece of paper, but hearing more of the story behind why that piece of paper was so important, Isaac now understood.

"I hate to admit this, but I feel like I owe you an apology," he said. "All this time, I've been judging you for having a silver spoon in your mouth, some snooty woman come from on high to tell us peasants how we ought to live. But you fought your way out of the trenches, just like me."

The smile Abigail gave him washed away all of his uncomfortable feelings. "I forgive you. The truth is, I owe you an apology. All this time, I have been despising you for lots of little things, and just this afternoon of getting to know you, I'm learning how wrong I was. So how about we both put the past in the past and move forward as colleagues, and maybe even friends?"

Her words humbled him, and he didn't know what to say. Usually when he apologized, it was met with a gruff acceptance. But Abigail only opened her heart further to him.

"Of course," he said. "I think we're both learning that neither of us is beyond having prejudices against people we don't know, even though this goes against so many of the things we've learned in school."

Abigail smiled, warming him. Strange how now that he'd gotten to know her, he could understand why people responded to her so well. In fact, he'd almost say he was attracted to her.

He'd once had that thought in class, when she was wearing this summery dress thing and he teased her that she looked like she was going to a tea party. And in that haughty way of hers, she'd said, "As a matter of fact, I am. My cousin arranged for us to go to tea at one of those old Victorian mansions, and I won't have time to change after class."

At the time, he'd seen it as a sign of how different their worlds were, but now seeing her in her element, he realized it probably was a really special and big deal for her. He almost wished he could go back in time to properly admire her, because from what he did remember she'd looked absolutely stunning. Even now, in faded jeans and a T-shirt, he still thought she was rather attractive.

Abigail stared at him like she'd asked him a question, and he shook his head. "I'm sorry. Were you saying something? I was lost in my thoughts."

Given that they'd just barely agreed to tread on common ground, it wouldn't be right to admit to her where those thoughts were. Besides, Abigail was the sort who wanted romance, marriage and happily-ever-after, and that wasn't something he'd ever be able to provide.

"I was just saying that earlier I was thanking God that he'd given us this opportunity to get to know each other better. He's clearly doing work in both of us through each other, and I'm so grateful for it."

Right. The other reason he wasn't a fan of Miss Abigail Shepherd. She was one of those Bible thumpers.

"Maybe," he said. "I don't give much credence to God arranging things for us in these good ways. After all, where was God when my father was beating me?"

He probably shouldn't have said that, considering a lot of their arguments in class were about God. Way to go and ruin everything when things were finally going right between them.

Argh. Abigail had forgotten that Isaac wasn't a believer. They'd had some pretty heated discussions in class about God's role in everything. Even though everyone here at the stables was a committed Christian who loved Jesus, because they worked with a public recreation center they weren't allowed to overtly teach religion. Abigail prayed for every single child who came through their door. Most of them would never know it, but she hoped that a little bit of God's love would rub off on them through her.

"I forgot that's a touchy subject with you," she said. "Don't worry, there won't be Bible lessons or anything here. We can't, since we work with a public rec center. I think we've pushed you on enough hard stuff. As for where God was when your father was beating you, I don't have an answer. I wish I did. But I do think that you were brought here for a reason, and that everything you've survived and thrived through means something more than just happenstance or accident."

Hopefully she wasn't coming off as being too preachy. But all she could do was speak from her heart and share what she knew. She'd learned that instead of wasting her time trying to figure out why certain things did or didn't happen according to what she thought was God's plan, she could only trust in Him. Just like with the realization that despite all of her prayers to be rid of Isaac, here they were. Though she wouldn't admit it to Isaac, she had a sneaking suspicion that God wasn't through with this part of his story just yet.

"I'm sure there are other explanations for it besides God," he said. "But things are going so well between us right now that I'm not going to try to argue with you over it. That, and I know where your heart is, and I know you mean well."

That admission was probably more touching than any other piece of conversation they'd had this entire time. She'd driven home from class one day in tears because of how he'd ridiculed her and her faith. The truth was, as much as she hadn't been able to stand him, she did have a bit of a crush on him because she thought he was kind of cute. So to have him make fun of her had been even more devastating. Of course, in their most heated arguments, when he'd acted like a total jerk, she'd always been able to forget about it.

Now, as those baby blues were looking at her with absolute sincerity, she wasn't sure what to do about the butterflies forming in her stomach. It wasn't like anything could come of her feelings. She was nearly twenty years older than him. They were at different stages in life. He was just starting out, and she was finding fulfillment in what she was already doing.

At her age, she'd given up on the idea of romance and love. Her work here was enough to satisfy her dreams of home and family. After all, she already had most of the desires of her heart. Her cousin and sister were back home, along with their families, and Abigail was getting to do everything she'd ever wanted, including earning her degree. Even if she sometimes wished to ask for more, it seemed almost selfish.

She led Isaac into the small kitchen that served as a break room for the staff. "You'll find that this is a fully stocked kitchen," she said. "Obviously, you want to label anything that's yours, but a lot of the things in the fridge, like condiments and such, are considered communal use. Some of the community members also bring us snacks and meals from time to time, so please feel free to help yourself to anything without a name on it. Just clean up after yourself and keep things tidy."

It felt much better to be back talking about professional things. Yes. That was what she needed to do whenever he gave her a look that made her heart skip a beat.

"I know you said you intended to commute, but in case you change your mind, let me show you what we have for you."

Abigail unlocked the door at the back of the kitchen. It brought them through a small hallway used for storage, and then to the efficient apartment they'd created for overnight guests.

"It's not much, but it's clean and comfortable," she said, gesturing at the small sitting area with a space divider for the bed area and the doorway into the full bath beyond. Just a few hours ago, she'd been agonizing over whether it would be up to Isaac's exacting standards, and now he might not use it at all. But as she gazed at her mother's quilt spread across the bed, with the afghan Josie had made folded at the end, Abigail felt a sense of pride at having done her best to make this a warm and welcoming space. Isaac walked over to the bookshelf.

"You weren't kidding about your reading taste," he said.

Abigail joined him. "No, but we did try to gather a variety, hoping we'd find something to your taste since we weren't sure what you liked."

Isaac spun to look at her. "Really?"

Abigail nodded. "Of course. We want you to feel as at-home as possible when you're here. It's how we treat all of our guests."

As Isaac ran his fingers along some of the spines of the books, something in his mood changed. "I've been in a lot of foster homes, and I'm used to being in places that aren't mine. But not a lot of people take the time to provide a variety to satisfy people's needs."

He pulled out a book on quantum physics. "Like this." He picked up another book, this time a book of jokes. "Or this."

"You couldn't stand me, but you did all this anyway?" he asked.

What was she supposed to say? This was what she'd have done for anyone. Though she'd admit she'd taken a little extra care to meet his needs so he wouldn't have anything to complain about.

"It's just what we do," she said. "It's not perfect. I mean, you would still have to use the communal kitchen, but we did put a mini fridge in here in case you had things you wanted to be sure you kept safe."

"I don't know a lot of people who are this kind to strangers, let alone someone they don't like."

Dare she step into the minefield?

"At the risk of starting an argument, the simple truth is that I'm only doing what God commanded us to do."

A sad look crossed his face. "Not all Christians believe that, you know. Maybe if more Christians were like you, I'd be one."

Abigail laughed. "I'm far from perfect. After all, I have totally confessed how judgmental I've been toward you. I'm a work in progress, but I do the best I can. And hey, just a few weeks ago, you were saying that Christians like me were everything that's wrong with the world."

It was weird, the way he was looking at her. Almost like—Abigail shook her head. No. He wasn't interested in her. That was foolish. Definitely time to get her mind on to other things.

"Anyway, if you ever have a long day and don't feel like making the drive, the space is reserved for you. Just let me know, and I'll be sure you have the key."

Her attempt at deflection didn't remove the expression from Isaac's face.

"You really are something special," he said.

She shook her head. "Stop. You're going

to give me an ego complex. I'm just doing what I'm supposed to do. Nothing more, nothing less."

Gesturing to the door, she said, "Let's get on with the rest of the tour. I wanted to show you the education area where people can learn a little bit more about horses, and then I can tell you more about your duties."

"Don't," Isaac said. "I am overwhelmed with your generosity of spirit, and you act like it's nothing. Take the credit. You're a remarkable woman, and you need to own that."

Was it getting hot in here? Though Abigail knew her sense of discomfort had nothing to do with the temperature of the room and everything to do with the man's gaze upon her, she still wanted to rush over and open a window.

But she'd made Isaac do a lot of hard things today, and as much as he wanted to give her credit for being a remarkable person, she was staring right back at one. But if she said that, he would only see it as her not taking credit again.

"Thank you," she said simply. "I don't get a lot of compliments like these, and I've always tried not to be prideful, so it's hard for me to accept such high praise. But I truly appreciate it, and I'm glad that I've been able to give you something special."

Isaac nodded, then gestured at the door. "Okay, then. I appreciate your honesty. So since we both made each other a little uncomfortable today, let's go ahead and finish the tour so we can get out of each other's hair."

Now that sounded like a great plan. The only trouble was they might get out of each other's hair for the day, but how on earth were they supposed to get through the summer?

Chapter Four

Even though Isaac spent a week in training before camp, at lunch on the first day,
Isaac couldn't remember a time when he'd
been more tired by noon. Interesting, since
he'd spent plenty of time working at Camp
Guffey. But he supposed it was a different
level of work.

Here, each staff member was in charge of
supervising the maximum number of camp
attendees because they were so tight on staff.
At Camp Guffey, they purposely kept the
numbers low, ensuring that each camper received individualized attention.

As he went to sit down, he spied one of the
kids sitting alone and apart from the others.

"Mind if I join you?" Isaac asked.

The kid didn't look up from his sandwich.
"I guess," he said.

Isaac's heart went out to the little boy. It was clear he didn't want to be there, and Isaac had noticed him standing off on his own more than once. This was only the first day of camp, so hopefully the boy would warm up to everyone soon.

As Isaac studied him, he noticed that in between bites of sandwich, he was reading a book.

"Good book?" Isaac asked.

The little boy sighed, then looked up at him. "Yes. And since this is the only time I get to read during this stupid camp, can you not talk to me and let me read my book?"

Ouch. So this kid was likely here against his will. His parents probably wanted him to go to summer camp, and they'd obviously chosen the wrong one. Isaac could relate. Sure, he'd enjoyed all the different camps and activities he'd gone to as a kid, but he'd be lying if he said that there hadn't been times when he'd been like this little boy, just wanting to get away and read his book.

Isaac glanced around, looking to see if there were any other children who might need some attention. He was tempted to leave so the boy could have the peace he craved, but as the next class got out and more children came running over to the picnic area, it wouldn't be long until this table was also full. At the very least, Isaac could provide a buffer for this child.

Abigail came over and sat next to him. "I see you've met Josh."

The boy grunted, acknowledging he knew he was being talked about, and Isaac smiled. "If you want to call it that," he said.

Abigail laughed, the gentle sound warming his heart. The more he got to know her, the more he wondered how he could have possibly disliked her so much in the past. She was a good woman, and he loved seeing her interacting with the children.

"Don't mind Josh," Abigail said. "I keep trying to tell his parents that he is never going to be a cowboy. He likes reading his books about dinosaurs, not horses. Every year, he comes for the summer because his parents want him to like horses."

Josh looked up from his book. "I'm sitting right here, you know," he said.

"I'm not saying anything that I wouldn't say to you," Abigail said. "I've said the same to your parents. But I thought it would be helpful to Isaac, since he's new here, to understand that it's not personal when you don't want to join in our activities or talk to us. I mean, sure, I'd love for you to participate because I think you're a pretty neat kid. But it's your choice, and I do what I can to respect it within reason."

Once again, Isaac appreciated the way she spoke to Josh like a rational human being who could have thoughts of his own. It always frustrated him that so many people thought they were connecting with a child by talking down to them. But Abigail's genuine love and compassion for the children was obvious in every one of her interactions.

"I don't know why you have to keep letting me come every year," Josh said, annoyance tingeing his voice. "You could tell my mom and dad I don't belong here."

Isaac had to smile at the frustration in the little boy's voice. How many times had he felt like a square peg trying to fit into a round hole? Nobody understood him, either.

"I'll tell you why," Abigail said gently. "Both of your parents work, and you're not old enough to stay home alone. There aren't any other affordable summer care options in our area. I made the same promise to you as I do every year. Participate the best you can, cooperate with your teachers on your lessons, and at the end of the summer, we'll find a fun dinosaur activity. You pick."

Josh's grudging smile and the tender way Abigail looked at him reminded Isaac a lot of his interactions with Mr. P. That first summer, Mr. P had made a similar deal with Isaac. If he did his best to participate and at least try all the activities, at the end of the summer, Mr. P promised to take him for a ride in his classic Corvette. At the time, Isaac had been crazy about anything on wheels, so even though he hadn't been much of a Corvette person, and still wasn't, that offer had made him feel like a million bucks. Like he was special and worth investing in. And even though city-kid Isaac had gone to the camp not wanting anything to do with the outdoor activities and sports, by the end of the summer, not only had he earned his ride in the Corvette, but he had also developed a love for a lot of the things he'd said he didn't want to do.

Isaac looked toward the paddock where the horses were grazing. Though he had been treating this whole situation as just something he needed to get through to earn his degree, maybe it was time to look at it as a deeper learning experience.

After all, Isaac had gone to Camp Guffey not even knowing how to swim, and to this day one of his favorite ways of reducing physical stress was going to a pool and doing a few laps. Just another gift Mr. P had given him.

Though he'd become much more comfortable around horses over the past week, he still hadn't been able to bring himself to go for a ride or spend any time with them other than when Abigail or one of the others made him. After lunch, they would be doing more to introduce the kids to the horses, and that was going to be the real test for Isaac.

Isaac looked at Josh and wondered if there was a way he could help him. After all the things Mr. P had done for him, helping someone like Josh was a start.

Isaac smiled at Josh. "Have you thought about what dinosaur activity to do?"

Josh shrugged. "Last time, we had someone come over and talk to us about the fossils he discovered on a local trail. I've been going hunting for dinosaur bones a lot, but I haven't seen any."

Isaac turned his attention to Abigail. "Have you done field trips to the different museums?"

Abigail nodded. "We have done some field trips, but going to see dinosaurs in the museum isn't something I can fit in the curriculum."

"What do you have against horses anyway?" Isaac asked Josh.

Josh slammed his book onto the table. "You people really just don't want me to read my book, do you?"

Isaac noticed that it was, in fact, a book about dinosaurs. And judging from the size and the look of the book, it was way more mature than he'd expected from someone of Josh's age. He must really like dinosaurs.

"I hate horses," Josh said. "My dad's horse kicked me once, and my dad just said to shake it off. Every time I get on a horse, I'm scared, and my dad and my brothers just laugh at me. I can't help it if I don't like horses. They don't like me much, either."

After seeing the pain and fear in the little boy's eyes, Isaac understood. Here was this dinosaur-loving kid born into a family of cowboys, and he didn't fit in. It must be hard, being afraid of horses in that context.

One more thing Isaac could relate to.

"I get it," Isaac said. "Can I tell you a secret?"

Josh shrugged. "If you want. You're not going to get me to like horses. Abigail has tried."

Tough kid, but Isaac got it. Kind of reminded him of the time that he was stuck with a foster family that was super into orchestra, and Isaac had never felt more misunderstood in his life. Thankfully, that placement hadn't lasted long because the family hadn't known what to do with a rowdy little boy who liked to destroy stuff while they wanted to sit quietly with their chamber music.

"I'm afraid of horses, too," Isaac said.

Josh looked at him suspiciously. "You're afraid of horses? You work at a horse camp. Why would you go to work in a horse camp if you're afraid of horses?"

All good questions, and Isaac chuckled. "The truth? I needed the job. Sometimes in life, to get what you want, you gotta do some unpleasant things."

The smile Abigail gave him warmed his heart. He could feel her supportive presence, would have felt it even if she hadn't been nodding approvingly. Isaac hadn't realized he'd needed her approval, but having her there gave him a deeper security than he'd thought possible.

Josh looked thoughtful for a moment, then smiled. "I guess so. That's what my dad always says. 'You gotta cowboy up and do what you gotta do.' I'm only ten years old, so it seems like a lot of doing what you gotta do before I ever get to do the things I love."

So much wisdom from such a little boy, and as Isaac glanced at Abigail, he saw the pain in her eyes. Sympathy for Josh or something else?

"I'm still scared of horses, though," Isaac said. "Even though Abigail's been helping me, I'm still kind of scared. Do you think you could be my buddy, and when we're doing horse stuff we could be scared together?"

Another suspicious glance from Josh. "You're really scared of horses?"

Isaac nodded. Every day, after staff training, Abigail had taken him to work with Simba to help him feel more comfortable. Though he did feel more comfortable around the horse, and understood more about horse safety, he wasn't about to jump on one anytime soon.

"No offense or anything, but you're kind of a big guy, and I'm just a little boy. You're bigger than my dad, so you shouldn't be scared of nothing."

"Size doesn't have anything to do with fear," Isaac said. "I've seen all the little girls here jumping around on the horses like they were nothing."

Josh rolled his eyes. "Great. Now you're like my dad, calling me a little girl because I am afraid of horses."

"Whoa, whoa," Isaac said. "That's not what I'm saying at all. First of all, there is nothing wrong with being a little girl. Secondly, you missed my point. There are people of all shapes and sizes doing things with the horses. We're different sizes, and we're afraid of horses. A person's size doesn't matter."

Abigail shifted nervously, like she thought Isaac was straying too far off course. But Isaac felt that way about size in all matters, not just horses. A person's heart was what was important to him, but that was probably way too much lecturing for the time being.

Isaac turned his attention back to Josh. "So can we make a pact? Any time one of us is feeling scared, just give the other a sign. I'll see that you're scared, and we'll know to be there for each other. That way, we both know it's okay to be scared and we don't feel so alone."

"So like a handshake?"

Isaac nodded. "Like a handshake, only I think this will be a hand gesture because sometimes we won't be next to each other. We just need to know we're there for each other, even across the room. That way we don't have to make a big deal of it so everyone knows we're scared."

He could sense the little boy's cautious optimism. "But I would know we're scared, right?"

Isaac nodded. "Absolutely. It's just between us. I mean, Abigail will know, but I think we can trust her."

Josh nodded and looked at Abigail. The warm smile on her face made Isaac regret every bad thought he'd ever had about this woman. It was clear that she deeply cared about every child who entered the property, and Isaac felt so blessed to know her.

"My dad says real men don't get scared."

Isaac nodded slowly. "That may be true for your father, and I would never ask you to disrespect him. I think it's not so much about being scared or not scared, because everyone is scared sometimes. It's just a matter of how you handle that fear. So now we have a way of handling our fear together."

For a moment, Isaac thought about what he could do to help Josh not feel scared.

"So here's what we're going to do," Isaac said. "Any time one of us feels scared, we catch the other person's eye, and we scratch our nose. Then, to acknowledge we saw that the other person is scared, we give a thumbs-up. No one watching us will know anything. If they see us, they just see us giving a thumbs-up. No one has to know what it means."

Abigail smiled at them both. "I love that. You don't mind if I join in with you, do you? Anytime you need that reassurance from me, you do the same thing. I'll give you a thumbs-up, too."

Josh looked at him, then at Abigail, then nodded. "All right," Josh said. "I'll give it a try."

A group of kids came running over to the table and plopped down with them. The boisterous laughter brought a lightness to the atmosphere, at least until Isaac saw the expression on Josh's face.

"Now can I read my book?" Josh asked.

Isaac laughed, and Abigail laughed with him. It felt good to be sharing this moment with her. Like they were a real team.

"Yes," Abigail said. "Read your book."

The look Abigail gave him made Isaac feel like he was part of something special. He always thought that that special feeling was something he'd gotten from Camp Guffey and Mr. P, but now he was starting to think that perhaps it was available to him in other ways and other places.

Abigail couldn't believe the interaction they'd just had with Josh. This was his third summer here at the camp, and Abigail was struggling with figuring out a way to get him to participate. True, it was only the first day, but usually on the first day, she'd been able to get Josh excited about something. As much as they had wondered if Isaac's fear of horses would be a detriment, she could now see that having one of the counselors terrified of horses might actually be a good thing. How many other children did they encounter who were afraid of horses? Abigail had always thought that the best way to handle it was to show them there was nothing to be afraid of, but maybe the thing these kids needed the most was to see people behaving bravely in spite of their fears. To acknowledge those fears and move forward anyway.

It was hard to believe what an encouragement and inspiration having her former worst enemy as a co-leader was. Who would have thought she'd be so thankful for his presence?

Isaac had turned his attention to one of the other campers, getting to know him so Josh had some time for his book. She'd have to look for some new dinosaur books for the rainy day library. Usually, she had the kids do an indoor horse-related activity or read a horse book, but her heart went out to the little boy who hated horses, whose parents kept trying to turn him into a horse lover.

One more thing she respected about Isaac. He also tried to meet the boy where he was at, and he understood that while not all kids were a fit for the horse camp, they had to find a way to make sure the misfits still felt cared for and included.

No wonder his goal was to run a camp of his own. It was too bad Isaac was so sold on this Camp Guffey place because they could use him here. But she also understood. As a former foster child, he wanted to help foster children. They were both helping the communities they'd grown up in, and she couldn't fault Isaac's choice to leave.

As lunchtime came to a close, Abigail helped the children clear up their messes, then gathered her class and directed them to the stations they had set up to allow the children to ease back into the day and learn more fun horse facts.

It also gave the staff time to connect with the children on a more personal and individual level, since they were all in small groups. Usually they already had the groups chosen and divided, but seeing the way Josh hovered near Isaac, she made a quick adjustment on her clipboard to put Josh in Isaac's group. Usually, she had to force Josh to participate, so this was amazing progress. Once again, she thanked God for Isaac being there.

Once the groups were finished, Abigail clapped her hands and brought everyone back together. "Now that we've all explored at our stations and learned something about horses, I want each of you to tell me what you've learned."

They sat around in a circle, and each child shared something fun they had learned. With the help of Maddie, Kayla's mom, the seniors at the senior center where she worked had put together some permanent displays in the stables as a way for the kids and anyone passing through to learn basic facts about the horses. The seniors loved having projects like this to contribute to, and it kept them active in the community. Going through the displays was always a great first-day activity for the kids. They could explore and test their knowledge as Abigail got a feel for each child and their distinct personalities.

Unsurprisingly, Josh opted not to share what he'd learned. The little boy often hung as far back as possible and only participated when Abigail forced him to. She wasn't going to put him on the spot this time, since he'd already moved further out of his comfort zone than ever.

When each child who wanted to had the chance to share, Abigail said, "Now it's time to take a walk through the stall area and meet the horses."

As they strolled through the barn, where the horses were in their stalls, Abigail gave her familiar speech about the horses and their different personalities. They'd already had their safety lecture, which was the very first thing they did with all the children at camp, but it was important to constantly and consistently reinforce the idea of being safe around horses.

When they got to the end of the stable block, Abigail looked back and noticed that Isaac and Josh had stopped in front of Simba's stall. Isaac had bent down to say something to Josh, and Josh howled with laughter. She'd never heard the little boy laugh like that before. He'd always been a serious and somber child, and the only way to engage him was to mention dinosaurs, and even then, Abigail always felt at a loss because she simply didn't have the kind of dinosaur knowledge that Josh did, and he seemed to have disdain toward anyone who didn't have that passion at his level.

Funny, as much as Josh's parents thought that he was picking up nothing from them, he was a lot like his dad in that if someone didn't fall in line with his way of thinking, he kind of shut down. She caught Isaac's attention and motioned for him to join them because they were moving on, and Isaac gave a small nod, but held up one finger. He was asking her to wait, and wanting to respect whatever was passing between Isaac and Josh, Abigail nodded and gave him a thumbs-up. He gave her a thumbs-up back, and then she turned her attention back to the class.

"You got to learn things about the horses, so let's talk about why we're here. I know some of you are really eager to ride the horses. We'll get to that in just a little bit," Abigail said. "But is there anything else you are hoping to get out of being here at camp?"

It felt so natural, asking that question, so much so that Abigail wondered why she hadn't ever asked kids that before. Usually she just assumed that they fell into one of two groups. The kids who loved horses and just wanted to be around them, and kids like Josh who were absolutely terrified of them, but whose parents thought it would be a great experience. It was usually easy to pick the extremes out, but for the first time, Abigail wondered about those who were kind of in the middle. What about them? Was she meeting their needs?

Having Isaac here was giving her a new perspective on the work she did. She'd been grateful that the internship program allowed people to use their current jobs for internship credit, and it was heartening to realize that she would be learning just as much from him as she hoped he was learning from this experience.

Katie raised her hand. Kids like Katie

were the reason Abigail was so committed to growing the camp and making it accessible for as many children as possible. Her family could barely afford the riding program, which was made affordable by the work of countless volunteers. But for licensing purposes, the camp needed to have a staff-to-camper ratio that they couldn't provide without a paid staff. Which meant the cost of the camp was beyond the reach of people like Katie's family. Instead of going to camp, she'd had to stay with their elderly neighbor, who didn't have a clue as to how to entertain a child Katie's age. However, thanks to all the work Abigail, Josie and Laura had done in getting grants for the camp, they could provide scholarships so kids like Katie could attend.

Abigail was so grateful they'd been able to make it happen for this little girl. If everything went well this summer, they could help even more kids.

"I've loved horses all my life," Katie said. "Getting to come here is the best thing that's ever happened to me!"

Abigail smiled. Abigail had known Katie her whole life, and a truer statement had never been made. Even as a toddler in the church nursery, Katie was jumping on someone's back and saying giddyup.

As the other kids took turns talking about why they were here, Isaac and Josh rejoined the group. Josh nudged Isaac, and Isaac bent down to speak to the boy.

Then Josh raised his hand.

"Yes, Josh? Why are you here?" Abigail asked.

Josh squared his shoulders. "I'm only here because my parents made me come. I don't like horses, and they don't like me. I don't see how they could be much use to me because when I grow up, I'm going to be a paleontologist."

With that, he scratched his little nose and looked over at Isaac, who gave him a thumbs-up.

That was probably the bravest thing Josh had ever said, growing up in a small town where everyone seemed to be interested in horses.

The best part about Josh's confession was a couple of the other kids murmured agreement that they were only here because their parents made them come, too. And suddenly, as those kids made eye contact with Josh, Josh could see that he wasn't alone.

Isaac was absolutely brilliant.

Getting Josh to talk about his discomfort in being here opened up the floor for others to share that they didn't want to be here, either, and now Abigail could see the ones who would need some extra TLC.

"You want to be a paleontologist?" Katie asked, a combative tone in her voice.

Josh stared at her, squaring his shoulders again. "Yes. So?"

Katie stared him down. "That's people who study dinosaurs, isn't it?"

Josh nodded, fear filling his eyes.

"Did you know that to get in the back-country places where the dinosaur bones are, sometimes the only way in is by horse-back?" Katie didn't let him answer and continued. "I went to a place where they used to dig dinosaur bones, and you know what they said? The expedition of people going to the dinosaur bones could only get there on horseback. Now what do you think of that?"

Katie was being extra sassy today, and Abigail tried not to laugh. She was torn between whether or not she needed to tell Katie to simmer down.

Josh scratched his nose, and Abigail gave him a thumbs-up.

"Is that true?" Josh asked.

"Are you calling me a liar?"

Josh shrank back.

Abigail turned to Katie. "I'm sure he's not calling you a liar, but this is new information to him. Why don't you tell us about this horseback expedition to find dinosaurs?"

Katie launched into a long explanation of everything she'd learned having gone to this dinosaur place. With her dad being a truck driver, sometimes in the summers he'd take her with him on his runs, and if they had time, they'd stop at sites like this dinosaur place.

When Katie was finished, Josh looked at her with almost a level of begrudging respect. "I didn't know all that about dinosaurs," he said. "Or that horse people liked them."

"I love horses *and* dinosaurs," Katie said enthusiastically. "My dad let me buy a book from the bookstore at that dinosaur place. If you want, and you promise to take care of it, I'll let you borrow it."

Josh lit up in a way Abigail had never seen before.

"Really?" Josh asked. "That would be awesome."

Katie squared her shoulders. "Good. And you can be my riding partner. We can talk even more about dinosaurs."

The terror on Josh's face made Abigail realize that while they'd made some amazing progress, Josh was probably not ready to be Katie's riding partner. The most daring of the children in her group, she wasn't likely to go easy on him.

"We'll discuss riding partners later," Abigail said. "First, let's go over to the horses we're going to be using for our camp and get to know them."

Isaac bent to say something to Josh, and Josh grinned, then went to sit by Katie. Abigail's heart swelled at the thought of the little boy making his first real friend in three years of attending camp. Maybe they couldn't be riding partners, but it was clear from the way Katie and Josh giggled, they were definitely going to be friends.

She'd debated about which class to put Katie in, since she was an advanced rider, and this class was all beginners, but the kids in the advanced classes were so much older than Katie that Abigail feared she wouldn't be able to make friends or fit in. This interaction made Abigail realize she'd made the right decision.

The way Isaac interacted with Josh made Abigail feel things she hadn't felt in a long time. It was as if her senses were on high alert, bringing new sensations that touched her in a very deep way. It was silly to have such feelings.

Oh yes, she understood the signs of attraction. But a young, handsome man like Isaac couldn't possibly be interested in a woman like her. And no, this wasn't Abigail being down on herself for not having proper self-esteem. It was the reality of coming from a different generation, having different life experiences and different needs for the future. A man like Isaac had hopes and dreams for his future, things Abigail couldn't provide.

It was just a silly schoolgirl crush. Yes, that was it exactly. She'd read enough books on adolescent emotional development that she knew she'd skipped half of the important stages. She'd been so busy raising her sister and cousin that she hadn't taken time for herself. She hadn't noticed the cute boys in her classes at school or who came around the stables. Especially not the ones who came around the stables. Not only would

her uncle Joe discourage her from frater-
nizing with their clients or employees, but
it also just made logical sense. After all, a
romance gone wrong would be terrible for
their business.

Which was why she absolutely had to
shove all thoughts of Isaac out of her mind.
Romance with him wasn't just a bad idea because of their age difference as well as their
differences of opinion on things like that.
It would be completely unprofessional for
them to have any kind of romantic attach-
ment. Especially since any feelings would be
completely on her side, and not his.

If only her heart didn't disagree with the
logic her mind kept coming up with. But
what else was she supposed to do? She could
crush on Isaac all she wanted, but nothing
could come of it.

Chapter Five

As Isaac plopped down onto the porch swing at the main ranch house, he had to admit he'd never been so tired. He'd worked a lot of camps for kids, but midway through the first week of camp, he'd usually acclimated. He wasn't looking forward to the drive back to Denver.

Abigail sat next to him and handed him a glass of lemonade.

"It looks like you could use this," she said.

He accepted the glass gratefully and took a long swig of the refreshing drink. "This tastes homemade," he said.

Abigail smiled. "It is. It's my specialty."

Isaac shook his head slowly. "I don't know how you have the energy to do all of this with the kids and still find time for homemade lemonade."

She gave him a warm, tender smile. "I guess I don't know any different," she said. "Uncle Joe never liked anything to be store-bought, and he was a bit of a miser, so everything had to be homemade if we wanted it. And the truth is, I enjoy doing it. For me, there's nothing so satisfying as squeezing the lemon and getting all the juicy goodness out of it. It's also nice because I can control the amount of sweetener in it. To be perfectly honest, I think that the stuff you get at the store or a restaurant is way too sweet."

"I would agree with that," Isaac said. "You've said that you raised your sister and cousin, and I guess I didn't realize all that it entailed. You helped them, sure, but it sounds like you also did all the cooking for the family as well."

Abigail nodded. "Well, what else was I going to do? We did have housekeepers off and on, but Uncle Joe was difficult to get along with, so most of them didn't last long. Especially in a small town like ours, his persnickety ways were well-known. Everyone respected him as a horseman, but when it came to help around the house, no one was willing to put up with his demands for long. It was okay, though, because I figured out how to take care of everyone. I'd get up early enough to make a simple breakfast of scrambled eggs and toast, pack everyone's lunches, which was just a sandwich, some chips and a piece of fruit, and sometimes, when I had time to bake them, even a cookie. I never made fancy dinners, but they were good, and they were filling."

"That sounds like an awful lot of responsibility for a child," he said.

Abigail shrugged. "I was a teenager. Not really a child, but you're right, not exactly an adult either."

"Have you ever thought about leaving?"

Abigail stared at him like he'd committed an unpardonable sin. "Leave? Why would I do that?"

He gestured at her phone. "Your lock screen is a beach scene, and your office has all kinds of pictures of travel. Have you ever been to those places?"

Abigail shook her head. "No. I'd like to, someday, but it's like every time I think about planning a trip for myself, something always goes wrong here at the stables. And to be honest, I don't want to travel alone."

It was strange to him, the way she talked about all of these things as though it was just a given that she couldn't have them. Plenty of people who had ranches or ran camps found time to take a vacation.

He glanced at the pickup truck that had just pulled in. Laura was getting her twin boys out, and Wyatt had rushed over to help with the baby.

"It seems like you have plenty of help now," Isaac said. "I noticed an invitation to a wedding in Costa Rica on the staff fridge. You wouldn't be alone there. Your family could take over for a week for you to go."

"Them?" Abigail said, laughing. "I couldn't ask them to take over running the stables so I can go have fun. They have three children under the age of two, and Josie has a teenager and a newborn. As it is, I'm constantly helping them."

She paused for a moment, looking so wistful it almost broke his heart. "As for the wedding, I'd love to go. But it's in the middle of camp season. We barely have enough staff to meet the state requirements to maintain the adult-to-camper ratio. It's fine. I've learned to accept that I have to turn down all summer invitations. This is the life I signed up for, so I take the good and the bad."

Through the way she spoke of it, it was

clear Abigail didn't see her actions as being a sacrifice. But Isaac had to wonder, when would Abigail get her turn?

"And what about you? Who takes care of your needs?"

"My needs? That's not their responsibility. I've always taken care of myself."

It was so strange how Isaac had always seen Abigail as a spoiled woman with a silver spoon in her mouth. Though he'd already learned so much about her to disprove that idea, talking with her now, he saw just how wrong he'd been. Not only was Abigail not a spoiled little rich girl, she was an amazing, self-sacrificing woman who had spent her entire life in service of others. And though he was angry that her uncle would allow a child to make such sacrifices and that, even now, her family couldn't see just how much she'd given up for them, it was clear that Abigail didn't have that resentment. She simply saw it as something normal and expected.

Taking care of herself came last, if at all.

Strangely, part of him wished he could find a way to take care of her.

It was on the tip of his tongue to ask her about romance and romantic attachments. Did she date? Had she ever loved someone?

But he dismissed those ideas as being none of his business.

He'd probably already crossed the line by digging this far into her personal life as it was. And yet, the question burned inside him. Her answers were more important than he would have thought. Because the other question on his mind was if she would ever consider going on a date with him.

Where did that come from? Him? Ask Abigail on a date? It wasn't that he was opposed to dating her, because she was a beautiful woman, and she was smart, funny and had a warmth and depth to her that he hadn't encountered in any of the women he'd ever dated. The truth was Isaac didn't date much himself because he found it difficult to relate to most of the women he met.

Abigail was the first woman he'd met who he could talk to, really talk to, and despite their rocky start, she was the first who truly tried to understand him.

Some people might think he was foolish to find a woman so much older than him so interesting. But the way he saw it, age was just a number. After all, Mr. P was nearly eighty, and he was one of Isaac's best friends.

He'd never gotten along with his peers,

and one of his foster mothers had told him that he was an old soul. Maybe that was true. When he looked at Abigail and spent time with her, all he saw was this incredible human being that he connected with in a way he'd never connected with anyone else before.

He could see himself falling in love with a woman like Abigail. But he was only here for the summer. Their life paths were taking them in different directions. As committed as she was to her family, he was to Camp Guffey.

That, and if he were really honest, he'd seen the dysfunction in his family and he feared being like his father—hurting the ones he loved. If Isaac truly loved someone, he couldn't risk losing his temper and causing them harm.

Following this attraction would only lead to heartbreak for them both.

He turned his attention back to the truck that had pulled up and watched as the twins came barreling toward them, finally free from the truck.

"Bee!" they yelled in unison.

Abigail went to greet them, wrapping her arms around the two precious children. The woman loved her family. His throat tightened at the thought because the more time he spent here at the ranch, the more he understood that love wasn't about blood. It wasn't about whose last name you had or didn't have, but about choosing to accept people for who they were and giving them your heart.

Wyatt came over and sat next to him, holding the baby.

"A full day with all those rugrats, and Abigail still has energy for mine," Wyatt said, chuckling.

"I was thinking the same thing," Isaac said. "To tell the truth, I am not looking forward to getting on my bike and riding home tonight. I'm exhausted."

"So spend the night," Wyatt said. "We've got the guest quarters for you. And there's always plenty extra dinner, so don't feel like you're imposing by sharing a meal with us. You're about the same size as Brady, so I'm sure he's got something that will fit you, clothes-wise."

Then Wyatt glanced over at the drink Isaac had been sipping. "Is that Abigail's lemonade?"

Before Isaac could answer, Wyatt held the

baby out to him. "Hey, you wouldn't mind holding Cash for me for a few minutes, so I can go in and get some for me and Laura?"

Wyatt didn't wait for a response but got up and went into the house. Isaac stared at the baby. The baby stared back at him. Great. What if he did something wrong? This was the first baby he'd ever held, and so far, it seemed to be going okay, except the baby kind of stared at him like he was expecting Isaac to say or do something.

Clearly Wyatt trusted him with his kid and thought he knew what he was doing, so he guessed it was going to be okay. He just held the baby in his arms, the way he'd seen the others do, and the baby didn't cry, so Isaac took that as a good sign.

"So, how you doing, little guy?" Isaac asked.

The baby continued staring at him. Okay, so not much of a conversationalist.

"What did you do all day?" Isaac asked, figuring he'd try again since he didn't know what else he was supposed to do with the kid. "Did you put anything interesting in your mouth?"

Abigail rejoined him, twins in tow. "Look

at him. You two are getting along just fine. Who knew you were also a baby whisperer?"

"I guess," he responded. "But I'll be honest, I have never done this before, so it's a little weird."

"You've never held a baby before?" Abigail gave him a funny look.

"Nope. I was placed in homes with older kids, and they never thought it was a good idea to put babies in with a bunch of teenagers. I don't have a lot of friends, and certainly not ones with kids."

The bright smile Abigail gave him made him feel like a million bucks. "Well, you're doing great," she said. "I think he likes you."

Imagine that. Isaac couldn't help the grin that filled his face. He was sure he looked like a total goofball, but it felt kind of nice to have such high praise from someone who knew what they were talking about.

He glanced around, noticing Laura and Wyatt's truck was gone. "Where's Laura? I think Wyatt was going to get them both some lemonade."

Abigail leaned over and gave the baby a tickle under his chin. "This little guy kept her up all night because he's teething, and no one took their naps today, so she is worn out. I sent her home to rest."

Isaac stared at her. "But you had a long day running the camps. Don't you need rest, too?"

Abigail laughed as one of the twins came running up to her with his toy truck. "Everyone has a full plate, but it's lighter when we all help each other. The good news is tonight I'm going to bed in my nice, quiet house with no crying babies. Laura doesn't have that luxury, so if I can help her out by watching the boys for a couple hours so she can get a little rest, I don't mind."

Wyatt came back out onto the porch, carrying two glasses of lemonade. "Where'd Laura go?"

Abigail explained what she'd just told Isaac, and Wyatt shook his head slowly. "Now, how did you get her to agree to take a nap? I have been bugging her ever since I got done with the camp, and she told me I needed my rest, too. I feel bad because I didn't even hear her get out of bed. I didn't realize she'd been up all night with the baby until I saw her looking haggard in the living room."

Then he chuckled and turned his attention

to Isaac. "Pro tip. When your wife is up all night with the baby, do not tell her she looks haggard in the morning. Probably best not to ever tell her that."

Wyatt laughed for a minute, then Isaac said, "No worries on that account. I'm not ever having children."

Abigail and Wyatt stared at him.

"Why are you not ever having children?" Wyatt asked.

Isaac shook his head. "First of all, we don't know enough about the whole nature versus nurture and what kind of genes we're passing on, and I know what I got from my family. I don't want to harm some other child with those genes. Second, as much as I am in this work to help kids, I struggle with wondering what kind of dad I'd be. However, if I decide to be a parent, there are so many kids in the system who need someone to love them, and who need a good home, I'll take in someone from the system. I don't need some kid carrying around my DNA, so why not give a child a home?"

Then Isaac shrugged. "It's all speculation anyway. To have a family, a man's gotta find a wife. And I don't know any women who share my passion for the kids and for the camp, knowing that my dream is bigger than my own personal happiness."

Suddenly, Isaac understood where Abigail was coming from. She had talked about sacrificing her life for her family. He was doing the same thing, only it was for a bunch of kids who needed to know that someone out there had their back. Once again, it struck him just how alike he and Abigail really were.

"You're young yet," Abigail said. "You might change your mind one day about having a family of your own."

Funny thing for her to say, considering how she has been spending her life. He stared right back at her. "I could say the same for you," he said. "After all, now that everyone's back here at the stables, there's nothing stopping you from having a family."

The look Abigail gave him was strong enough to melt glass.

"I've got almost twenty years on you, so I know when that ship has sailed. But you still have plenty of time to find someone to love you and have a family with."

Isaac shook his head. "Honey, if you think I am changing my mind on this, then you haven't gotten to know me as well as you seem to think. I do not want children of my own."

Then he shook his head. "No, that's not true. I do want children of my own. I feel like the children I work with are my own. Biological children? I can assure you that will never happen."

The baby in his arms let out a wail as if he objected to Isaac's strong speech.

"Oh, I'm sorry. I didn't mean to upset the baby," Isaac said.

"He's just teething," Wyatt said. "Give him a little bounce on your knee, and he'll be fine."

A car pulled up, and Kayla got out, followed by a frazzled-looking woman. This must be Maddie, Kayla's mom. He hadn't met her yet, but he'd heard enough about her to be reasonably sure this was who she was.

"Sorry we're late," the woman said. "Kayla has finally decided to get her license now that her friends have theirs, and she felt the need to take the long way around."

Abigail and Wyatt laughed.

"At least she is finally doing it," Abigail said. "Who would've thought that a trick rider would be afraid to drive a car?"

Kayla glared at her. "I trust my horse. I

don't trust any of the other weirdos on the road."

Everyone laughed and Wyatt held up the extra glass of lemonade. "Either of you want this? I got it for Laura, but Abigail managed to talk her into taking a nap because she was up all night with the baby."

Maddie took the glass from him. "Don't mind if I do. That was a nerve-racking drive up here."

"I didn't do anything scary," Kayla said, sounding indignant.

"No, but half the time I had no idea where you were going, and you know I hate being late."

Kayla shrugged as she took the baby out of Isaac's arms. "Baby time?" Kayla asked, laughing, but not waiting for a response. "We're going to get our own lemonade."

With that, she went off into the house.

Maddie sat in one of the chairs. "To tell the truth, driving with Kayla was terrifying. She only knows brakes or full throttle, and I'm not sure my nerves can take much more of this."

"Maybe a fresh driving partner would give her a different perspective," Isaac said. "I'd be happy to help her."

Maddie looked at him. "I haven't met you yet."

He smiled, walked over to her and held out his hand. "Isaac Johnston. I'm the summer intern here at the stables, helping Abigail out."

Maddie nodded slowly. "Aren't you a tall drink of cool water," she said. "Abigail told me about you, but not that you were pretty darn cute. Interesting detail to leave out."

Then she looked over at Abigail, giving her a sly look. "I smell romance in the air."

Abigail's face heated at Maddie's words. She had just come to terms with the idea that she might possibly have a crush on Isaac, and now Maddie had to point it out. She said a quick prayer for patience and then said, "Well, your romance meter is off. We have a strictly professional relationship, so don't be getting any ideas."

Maddie took a sip of her lemonade. "I said what I said."

Abigail stole a glance at Isaac. Were her words enough to make him understand that she wasn't interested in him? And why would Maddie say such a ridiculous thing? Hopefully if he believed Maddie, he'd see it as only a harmless crush and not make it weird.

After an uncomfortable silence, Wyatt cleared his throat. "Now Maddie, we will not interfere with anything that may or may not be happening between the two of them.

Abigail wasn't sure whether to be encouraged or discouraged by those words. Was Wyatt advocating a romance between them or was he trying to cool it down? At least they were stopped from having to answer by Brady and Josie walking up with their baby.

"Are we the last to get here?" Brady asked.

Abigail laughed, trying to dispel the odd energy around them. At least this was a safer topic. "Yes," she said. "And I'm starving. So let's get inside and eat."

Once in the house, it felt good to be back in some semblance of their normal routine. Normal, with the exception of Isaac, who had grown strangely quiet after Maddie's comments about romance being in the air. Hopefully, this wasn't going to ruin everything. It was just starting to feel like they'd come to a place of understanding one another and being able to be friends. Had Maddie's question ruined it all?

As they all gathered in the kitchen, the familiar routine brought more comfort to Abigail. Family members got out dishes and set the table as others brought out the salad fixings. She took the roast and vegetables out of the slow cooker to arrange them on a platter.

Isaac came up next to her. "It looks like everything is covered, but is there anything I can do? It seems like a well-oiled machine here."

Abigail smiled. "That's because it is. Obviously, we added family members over the years, but what makes our family work is that everybody pitches in and works together."

She looked at him for a long moment, remembering the way he quizzed her earlier about everything she did for the family.

"I know you look at what I've done as being a big deal and a huge sacrifice, but it isn't like I ever did it alone. Yes, I did the primary things to get the meals ready and have people taken care of. But never discount the fact that we all pitch in and work together."

She opened the drawer to get the serving utensils needed for today's meal. "Please put these on the table while I finish plating all of this."

Isaac did as he was asked, and she hoped

that the small lesson made him realize that none of the things she'd ever done had been a sacrifice. This was what families did. They all worked together and contributed for the greater good. On the porch, he'd made her seem like a martyr or something, but that wasn't it at all.

But as she spied Brady steal a kiss from Josie and saw the way Josie's face lit up, she couldn't help wishing that she'd find a love like that for herself.

Was it greedy of her to ask?

Please, God, I know I have been given so much already, but if it's possible, could I have someone to love?

After everyone had gathered at the table and they said grace, Abigail looked around with satisfaction at her family. Sure, it had been hard getting here, but the joy she received in simple moments like these made everything worth it. If God didn't answer her prayer for love, she had everything she needed. Even if she did feel a little lonely sometimes.

Sharing a meal together made everyone relaxed. It seemed that the tension from earlier with Maddie and her romance comment had all been forgotten, and everyone returned to normal. If a person's heart could smile, that's what Abigail's would be doing right now as she listened to everyone sharing about their day. Even Isaac relaxed and joined in. The truth was, even though Maddie's comments had hit a nerve, she wasn't wrong. Abigail liked Isaac, foolish as it was. And seeing the way he fit in with her family made it even harder.

How was she supposed to not fall for someone who had so easily fallen into their routine? A lot of people didn't understand why an extended family would choose to share so many meals together like this and live on the same property. Though obviously that closeness did have its limits, considering they all had their own separate homes.

Sometimes space was good, and that was what made the family so special. They understood how to balance these things, and they'd learned how to work through their issues.

After dinner, her family retreated to the barn to look at something Brady was making. But Isaac hung back.

"No fair for them to stick you with the dishes," he said. "But since I didn't do much in getting things set up, let me take care of it, and you relax for a little bit."

Tears stung the back of Abigail's eyes at his words. She was silly to get teary-eyed over something so small, but as much as Abigail helped everyone else, no one had ever offered to take over Abigail's chores simply so she could relax.

Isaac asked her earlier who took care of her, and she'd confidently told him that she took care of herself. If she were honest, deeply and truly honest, sometimes she did wish that somebody would take care of her for a change.

She swallowed the tears that threatened. This was just silly talk. Everyone knew that Abigail's job was to take care of everyone else, and after all these years, it was wrong to wish for something different. Besides, if Abigail had said, "Hey, could you give me a hand with the dishes?" every single one of them would have said yes. Abigail simply didn't ask, and no one ever offered.

"That would be great, thanks," Abigail said. "No one ever offers to do the dishes. After all, it's the most tedious chore."

Isaac shook his head. "I disagree. I like doing the dishes. I'm terrible in the kitchen, so everything I cook is a disaster, and it seems like I mess up everything else I try to help with when I have kitchen duty. Doing dishes is a great way for me to contribute. Especially because you're right. Most don't like doing the dishes."

He hesitated, then continued. "You know, it's funny, I've wondered about your unorthodox family. I've never seen one quite like it, and I can't help thinking that if more families were like this, the world would be a better place. What's your secret?"

Abigail watched as he searched for the dish soap. His openness was making it harder and harder to deny her silly crush.

"You probably aren't going to like my answer," she said. "But I don't have anything else to tell you. The secret to our family's closeness is God. I know it sounds trite, but the one thing that Uncle Joe did well in spite of all of his mistakes is he brought us to church every Sunday. He brought us around people who loved the Lord with all their heart. He was far from perfect, but this was something he did right."

Isaac stared at her. "How can you praise him as a man of God when he was such a terrible parent? I know you all say that you've forgiven him for the way you were raised, but that doesn't make him a man of God."

The pain in his voice made Abigail's heart ache. He'd clearly been hurt by someone in the church at some point in his life, but it seemed like, from their many conversations, he'd been hurt by a lot of people in a lot of ways. She couldn't imagine bearing that burden without knowing the love of God.

"I've never said he was perfect. I could list all of his flaws, including ones where he didn't live like Christ asked us to. But none of us do. We all fall short of the glory of God, and that is the beauty of God's love for us. We don't have to be perfect to be loved. He didn't live that message out. In fact, it was exactly the opposite. We thought we had to be perfect to be worthy of his affection, and everyone still fell short."

Tears filled her voice. She hadn't realized how heavily the subject weighed upon her, but when Isaac reached his hand out to touch her arm and comfort her, she shook her head.

"Please. Let me continue. Yes, it is true that our uncle lived out the opposite of what the Bible tells us about God's love, but that's just it. People on earth will always let you down. When I was a little girl, watching my mom die from cancer and seeing the guilt she felt at leaving us without a mother, the one thing she told me that I have carried in my heart ever since is that no matter how badly people let us down, God will always be there for us."

She wiped the tears from her eyes. "I have clung to the promise that she gave me on her deathbed my entire life. And it has never been wrong."

Abigail took a deep breath and reached for Isaac's hand. "Yes, people will let you down. People who say they follow God will let you down. But they are not God. And I can tell you with every ounce of my being that I have seen God come through for me time and time again. He is why my family is home."

She looked into Isaac's deep brown eyes and saw tears shining there as well. "You say that," Isaac said. "But when bad things happened, where was God? Why does He let all these bad things happen? Why would he allow kids like me and kids in worse situations to have the childhoods that they do?"

Abigail took a deep breath. "I don't know. But the thing is, God never promised us a life free from trouble. He just promised He would always love us, no matter what."

They stood there for a moment, not saying a word, but holding hands and looking deep into each other's eyes. How many people had promised to love Isaac, and let him down? Yes, Abigail had been let down by a lot of people, but she couldn't imagine the pain Isaac must have endured.

Isaac was the first to break the gaze, then he loosened his hands. "Is that why you all allow Maddie to be part of your family? Even though she's Brady's ex? I thought it was weird that Josie didn't seem to mind."

Abigail had been expecting this question at some point, but it was strange to be addressing it now. Still, maybe this would help. Briefly, she explained how Brady and Josie had been high school sweethearts, and everyone thought they were going to get married, at least until Maddie announced that she was expecting Brady's baby. Brady didn't remember the night he'd supposedly spent with Maddie, so he accepted baby Kayla as his own and raised her with Maddie. It wasn't until Josie came back recently that Maddie admitted in a fit of anger that she'd lied about the whole thing.

Kayla's father was someone she met at a party, and Maddie didn't even know who he

really was. But after a lot of counseling, a lot
of prayer and a lot of time with God, they all
agreed that Maddie's actions, while repre-
hensible, needed to be forgiven. She'd been
a young girl desperate for someone to love,
who got caught up in a lie and didn't know
how to get out. As part of that forgiveness,
they made her part of the family because
they all agreed that the most important person in the equation was Kayla. Kayla had
spent her whole life believing that Brady was
her father and loved him deeply, and Brady
loved her. It seemed only natural to include
Kayla's mother as well.

Isaac was silent as Abigail told the story,
and then he shook his head slowly. "That's
amazing," he said. "How could you forgive
something like that?"

Abigail shrugged. "Because God for-
gives her. God loves her. The thing is, as
we worked through all of this, the biggest
realization we all had was that, deep down,
Maddie never believed herself worthy of
love. She didn't understand that all these
terrible things she did didn't make her un-
lovable to God. And we chose to give her
that same love."

Isaac's eyes shone with tears. "I've done

a lot of bad things myself," he said. "Things I'm ashamed of. But if God could love Maddie after all the things she did, do you think he could love me?"

Abigail wrapped her arms around him. "I believe with all my heart that God loves you."

The warmth of his arms around her felt like coming home in a deeper way than she had ever experienced. Silly, considering she'd never left home, and she was currently at home. But in this moment in her kitchen with Isaac, Abigail had never felt more like she belonged.

Chapter Six

"Is it okay if I pray for you?" Abigail asked him.

Usually when someone asked Isaac if they could pray for him, he nodded and let them do their thing because he didn't want them to feel bad. But for the first time, Abigail's prayers were something he sincerely wanted.

Isaac nodded. "Please."

The confession Isaac had just made to Abigail was by far the number one thing he would have thought he'd never say. But no one had ever talked to him about God like that before. He'd never heard that God loved him unconditionally. It was always about how naughty he'd been and how bad he was and how he'd face God's punishment. Sure, he'd heard that God would forgive him of his sins, and on the rare occasion, he'd ask, but he never felt forgiven, and people never treated him like he had been.

But this family lived what they said they believed about God and gave forgiveness to a woman who had caused them harm, and not just by saying they forgave her, but by embracing her as a member of their family. Maybe, as much as he thought all this was such a mess, he really didn't understand things as well as he thought he had.

He'd always felt like an outsider, never belonging in any of the foster families he'd been a part of. So many of his foster siblings had taunted him for not being of their blood. But here, they accepted stepchildren, ex partners, and treated them all just as though they were blood relatives. Isaac had said earlier that if he had children, it would be foster children, but the truth was he didn't know how to make a bunch of unrelated people family. Even though it was one of those possibilities he'd kept in the back of his mind, it wasn't an idea he'd pursued seriously. But now that he could see the love this family had for each other, it was more than just an idea that could maybe happen; it was something he'd pursue as a reality. That is, if he could ever find a woman to love. A woman who would love him. But that was the thing. He opened his eyes and looked at the woman who was still praying for him.

Abigail was so beautiful. Not just in her appearance, but in the loving heart she showed, even to those who didn't deserve it.

Was it inappropriate to think of a woman in that way while she was praying? He didn't know. He was new to all this God stuff. Maybe it was wrong, but he couldn't help but feel that it was also very right.

"In Jesus's name, Amen." Abigail gave him a hug, and it took everything Isaac had to remember that this gesture was something Abigail did as an expression of compassion.

Despite what Maddie said earlier, Abigail hadn't given any indication that she felt anything more than friendship between them. He didn't want to ruin the tentative relationship they'd built by assuming anything more. Besides, he was leaving at the end of the summer, and Abigail's place was here. It wasn't fair for either of them to start something that couldn't go anywhere.

He looked up at her, and she smiled. "Thank you for trusting me with this," she said. "It's truly an honor to have you share your heart with me."

Okay, it was official. Abigail had to be the most amazing woman he'd ever met. Now his thought on never marrying has become 'how would he ever find someone like her'? She'd set a standard that he wasn't sure anyone could meet. He just wished he'd been able to become her friend earlier.

"I've spent so much time hating you, and I wish I had taken the opportunity to get to know you sooner," he said. "You are truly the embodiment of loving your enemy."

The small smile she gave him warmed his heart. "I could say the same for you," she said. "After all, enemies don't become friends in a one-sided situation. We both have learned to look past our prejudices, and I'm really grateful that you took that chance on me."

There were so many chances he wanted to take on this magnificent woman. As far as he was concerned, Abigail had the most beautiful heart he'd ever seen.

"It sounds like we finally did it right, though," Isaac said. "I know we're just supposed to be coworkers, but I hope you know that I now consider you a friend."

Friend. When he wanted so much more. But this was a good start. Someday…maybe? Or maybe sharing that thought would only ruin what they'd barely found. He'd rather have Abigail as a friend than not at all.

Her smile lit up her face, and he couldn't help thinking that she was prettier than any model's picture he'd ever seen. Everything about Abigail was genuine, and that made her the most beautiful woman in the world.

"I consider you a friend, too."

Phew. Okay, he needed a break from all this emotional stuff.

"I'd better get to those dishes," he said.

He went back to the sink. The water had gotten cold, but he dug his hands in and started scrubbing.

"You really don't have to do that," Abigail said.

"Yes, I really do. I told you, I like doing dishes. I know this sounds weird, but I want to feel like I'm a part of the family. I know you don't require it of me, but you have all given so much to me, I need to do this to give back. And, as I told you, this doesn't feel like a burden to me. I enjoy doing dishes."

He watched as her face softened when she finally understood, and it felt good to give her that, as well. He gestured at the living room.

"I know that your new book just came in the mail today. I overheard you telling Josie that she could borrow it when you're finished. Go sit and enjoy."

Abigail looked at him in surprise. "I didn't intend to do any reading until the weekend. I have to—" She gestured around the kitchen, then seemed to realize what he'd been trying to get her to do.

"Oh," she finally said. "If you're really sure, I could make us some tea, and there's some cookies."

Abigail, still trying to serve when he'd just given her the freedom to do something for herself.

"Do you usually drink tea and eat cookies when you're reading?"

The sly grin that filled her face made his stomach do a flip-flop. "I have a secret cookie stash just for that purpose."

Isaac laughed. "So you do know how to take care of yourself."

"Well…" The hesitation on her face made him laugh again. "I might have been known to share from time to time."

Of course she did. Because that's who

Abigail was. Always taking care of everyone else. Seeing her giving heart and how much she did for others made Isaac wish he could do more for her. He knew that if someone like him didn't step in to help, she'd never get all the things she wanted. Maybe it wasn't PC to say so these days, but she needed someone to take care of her the way she helped others. And as much as he kept fighting his feelings for her, what he really wanted was to be the man to do so.

Abigail felt almost sinful, sitting in her favorite chair with her new book. Isaac had insisted that she go sit and he'd make the tea and bring her some cookies. Decadent. For a moment, she could close her eyes and pretend that this was her life. Everything she'd ever dreamed of. Because, of course, in that dream, Isaac wouldn't just be doing all this to be nice or out of gratitude for how she'd helped him earlier, but because he loved her.

She could hear him fumbling in the kitchen, so she asked, "Do you need any help?"

"No, I've got it. You enjoy your book."

The back door opened, and Abigail could hear Josie and Brady say something to him. The three of them laughed, but before she could get up to see what was going on, Josie came into the family room.

"Don't you dare. Isaac is trying to do something nice for you, and you're going to let him."

Abigail sank back into her chair, and Josie noticed the book. "Besides, you need to hurry up and finish that book so I can read it."

She knew what Josie was trying to do. Josie had been bugging her to take more time for herself as well, but what Josie didn't understand was that if Abigail didn't do it, then it wasn't getting done. And yes, Josie would be the first to tell Abigail to ask for help, but Josie had a newborn, and she was running the office side of camp so she could have the baby with her. Josie had way too much on her plate to ask her for help.

"I'm trying," Abigail said. "But if you're all done at the barn, someone needs to watch the kids so Wyatt can get the truck and bring them home."

Josie groaned. "Brady and I just came in to get some drinks for everyone. We're going to watch the kids while Kayla takes Wyatt on the ATV to get his truck. It's handled."

Before Abigail could ask further questions about the arrangement, Isaac entered the room carrying a cup of tea and a plate of cookies.

"Sorry that took so long," he said. "I've never made tea that was loose like that. I just know how to stick a bag in a cup. Brady and Josie saw me trying to fish the leaves out of the water, so they showed me how to use the tea ball thing instead. Now I know for next time."

Abigail wasn't sure which made her heart beat faster—that Isaac would take the time to try to make her a proper cup of tea, or that he was already planning on there being a next time.

"This is wonderful, thank you." She smiled at him, hoping he didn't see the stars in her eyes.

Isaac returned her smile. "It was my pleasure."

Swoon! If she were twenty years younger, she'd be throwing herself at this man. All she could do now was take a sip of the tea he'd just brought her.

As soon as he left the room, Josie said, "It was the most adorable thing ever. He was trying so hard to make you a cup of tea the right way and not bother you with how he'd messed it up. I think he really likes you."

Argh. Not another one.

"That is sweet, but please… No more of this nonsense about Isaac liking me. It was bad enough, earlier, that Maddie made it sound like we could be an item. I don't need you on it as well."

Josie stared at her. "And why not? It's about time you found some happiness for yourself. I don't think I've ever seen you go on a date, and you deserve to have a little romance in your life."

"I don't disagree. Of course I would love to find Mr. Right. She inclined her head toward the kitchen. But Isaac isn't right for me. The age difference alone makes it seem impossible."

Instead of seeing the logic in Abigail's point, Josie frowned. "So what if you're older than he is? What matters is that the two of you have a real connection. I see the way you look at him, and the way he looks at you when he thinks no one is watching. There's something special there, and you owe it to yourself to pursue it."

She should have known that Josie wouldn't understand the impossibility of the situation. "But there's more than that. Isaac is leaving at the end of the summer, and I can't fault him for that. I wouldn't ask him to stay. I can't leave here, so how do you make a relationship work? Besides, though we made some really great progress today on his faith, the truth is we don't see eye to eye on a lot of important value issues. It seems like there's too much stacked against us. I'm not willing to risk the friendship that we've been developing on something with so little likelihood of success."

Josie looked at her intently. "It seems like you've given this a lot of thought for someone who's not interested in him."

Reasoning with her cousin was impossible.

Before Abigail could think of a decent comeback, Josie said, "We all see it. Sure, those seem like obstacles, but when I look at how easily I gave up on love with Brady all those years ago, I don't want to see you make the same mistake. Yes, it all worked out in the end, but you don't know if you're going to get a second chance, so take this one."

"I barely know him," Abigail said. "There's no comparison here."

Josie shrugged. "Fair. But it's clear that you both like each other, so why not at least give it a try and see what happens?"

Dishes clattered in the kitchen, reminding Abigail that Isaac could easily overhear their conversation. She lowered her voice.

"I don't want to talk about this. Not only is Isaac in the other room, but he's given me no indication that he's interested in me. We've finally gotten to the point of being friends, and I don't want to ruin what we've built by mistaking his kindness for something else. Please. I need you to respect where I'm coming from here."

Though Josie looked like she wanted to say more, she nodded. "All right. If that's what you really want. I hope you know that I'm on your side here. You've sacrificed your whole life for the rest of us, and it's only natural that we want you to be happy, too."

"I am happy," Abigail said. "I have everything I've ever wanted. My family is finally together again, and everyone is happy."

The sound of children's laughter echoed in the kitchen, followed by the deep rumble of men's voices. Kayla came into the living room.

"We're back." She glanced at the plate of cookies on the table beside Abigail and grinned. "Oh good. I need one of those. Have to build up my strength for Mom freaking in the passenger seat when we drive home."

Josie shook her head at her stepdaughter. "I don't think so. Those are Abigail's. Get your own."

Then she added, "And be nice to your mom. She's doing her best."

"I really need a cookie for that." Kayla reached for the plate again.

"I don't mind," Abigail said, noting that there were two cookies left. She'd have liked both of them, but she also didn't want to be greedy.

Once again, Josie shook her head. "But I do. Those are your cookies, and you deserve to have a break to enjoy them."

Josie gestured in the direction of the kitchen. "Now let's leave Abigail in peace to enjoy her book, and we can get everyone ready to go home."

Prior to Isaac's comments about Abigail's sacrifice, Abigail wouldn't have thought twice about this interaction. She'd thought that it didn't bother her to sacrifice for her family, but it also gave her a special thrill to realize that she didn't have to give up a cookie. Obviously Josie didn't think it was greedy, and she'd defended Abigail's right to have some time to herself.

Was it possible that many of the things

Abigail had denied herself were actually available to her? She'd always thought that she was following the biblical ideal of putting her family before her, but the women's group at church had been talking a lot about the importance of self-care. You couldn't fill a bucket from an empty well. At the time, Abigail had dismissed the idea, believing she had all she needed.

But as she bit into her cookie, she started thinking about what it would look like to have more.

She hadn't been lying when she'd told Isaac that her family would do things for her if she asked, so what would happen if instead of just thinking she had to do it all herself, she asked for help?

Sipping her tea, she could hear the others in the kitchen talking, and from the few words she'd caught, they were helping Isaac put away the dishes, since he didn't know where anything went. Abigail had assumed she'd have to deal with them later.

Isaac came back into the room. "We got everything taken care of. Is there anything else you need before we head out? I'm going over to see what Brady has for me to borrow to wear tomorrow, then I'll be putting that staff apartment to use."

"Thank you," Abigail said. "Tonight was a real treat. You made me realize that I don't often take time for myself, and I never ask, even though others are happy to help. So now I can spend the rest of the evening sipping my tea, finishing my cookies, and enjoying this book."

The smile he gave her warmed her to the tips of her toes. "You're welcome. I hope you know that you deserve all the love and care you tell us we're worthy of. You're just as worthy, and you need that same care."

Wow. Abigail had never thought of it that way. So many years, she'd thought doing these things for herself made her greedy or selfish. But Isaac was right, she would have told others that they deserved to have nice things and time for themselves so they could be their best for others.

Isaac turned to leave, but Abigail stopped him.

"Wait," she said. "I know that you're not so sure on all this God stuff, but I hope you know that God is using you in my life. Thank you for showing me that it's okay to take care of myself sometimes."

The look he gave her was warmer than the cup of tea she'd been sipping, and even more soothing. "You're welcome. I'm starting to think that maybe this God stuff isn't so bad."

As he left, the glow she felt deep inside intensified. No man had ever been so compassionate toward her. She thought of all the reasons she'd told Josie she couldn't be with Isaac, and as much as she hated to admit it, they were starting to sound like excuses.

But in the end, one thing remained.

Abigail wasn't willing to make a fool of herself and risk losing the friendship she'd just found.

Maybe Isaac was the best man she'd ever met. And he'd done more for her than any other man. But she had to believe that if this goodness existed, God had to have something just as good or even better for her. She just had to have faith.

Chapter Seven

Isaac finally gave up on the idea of commuting after the second week because as much as he hated to admit it, Abigail had been right that it was too much of a drive. But more than that, he found that he didn't like leaving everyone. Saying goodbye to Abigail at the end of the day was hard enough, but he was growing fond of the rest of her family as well. Isaac couldn't remember a time when he'd experienced more camaraderie and genuine friendship.

He smiled as he cleaned up after lunch, gladly taking Brady's turn on cleanup duty because Brady wanted to go and check on the baby. Isaac had never been part of a team like this, where it was a joy to do the dreaded tasks because you knew you were contributing to something greater than yourself.

As Isaac placed the last of the garbage into the trashcan, Josh came up to him.

"I found you some more trash," he said.

Isaac smiled at the boy. "Thank you, but you didn't need to stay behind and help. In fact, you should be with the class getting ready for your riding lesson. It's going to be so exciting, your first ride."

The look of terror on Josh's face made Isaac's heart hurt. He knew that look well. He imagined it was the same expression he'd had on his face in the past when he'd been asked to ride.

"My tummy hurts," Josh said.

He'd used that excuse the day before, and the day before that he'd spent time in the infirmary with a tummy ache as well. When his parents dropped him off today, they'd firmly told Isaac not to fall for that trick again.

But what else could Isaac do? If the little boy was really sick, Isaac would be responsible. Isaac held out his hand, grateful when Josh took it. "You know what your mom and dad said. So what am I supposed to do?"

Josh got teary-eyed. "My tummy really

does hurt," he said. "It's like there's a big T. rex eating the inside of my tummy, and it hurts real bad."

Isaac didn't doubt Josh's stomach hurt. It was common to have stomach pains when nervous or anxious or afraid. Regardless of whether or not he had an actual illness, the little boy was in pain. Telling him it was all in his head or forcing him to move forward wasn't the answer.

"I'm afraid of horses, too," Isaac said. "Let's go to the barn and see what we can figure out."

The boy nodded. "Yeah, I know. You told me."

"Sometimes having a friend go on the horse with you can help you not be so nervous."

Josh shook his head furiously. "No. Please don't make me go with Katie. Have you seen her ride? She likes to go fast, so I don't think that's a good idea."

Katie had befriended Josh, and when they weren't around the horses, the two children had great conversations about dinosaurs, but Katie hadn't been able to convince him to actually go for a ride with her.

As they got closer to the barn, the boy's

pace slowed. "Please don't make me do this," he said.

In good conscience, Isaac couldn't. Forcing a child to do something like this that he was terrified of—especially when you were dealing with a horse, who had a brain and made its own decisions—seemed like a terrible idea.

But the whole point was to get this child riding, which his parents had made very clear earlier today.

"What are we supposed to tell your mom and dad?"

Tears flowed down Josh's face. "Maybe I should run away. If I don't ride, my dad will be mad, but if I do, Gabe is going to make the horse kill me."

Wait, what?

"What's this about Gabe?" Isaac examined Josh's face, seeing the real terror, realizing that it was more than just a fear of horses.

"I wasn't supposed to tell." Josh took a step back. "Please don't say anything. He'll know I told, and he said that if I told on him, he'd make Katie's horse buck and Katie would get hurt."

Isaac guided Josh over to one of the benches

in front of the stable. At this point, they were beyond late for class, but this wasn't a situation you could brush under the rug.

"I won't say anything," Isaac said, hoping he could keep his word. "But you need to be straight with me about what's going on so I can help you. You don't need to be afraid of anyone here at this camp."

Josh scratched his nose, then said, "I trust you."

Progress. Isaac gave him a thumbs-up.

"When they rode the first day, Gabe was all braggy about how he was the best rider and he didn't belong with the little kids because he was an expert. Katie told him it wasn't nice to talk like that, and he said she was just a dumb girl. His horse took off on him, and when he tried to say it was on purpose, Katie said that if it was, it was the worst control and form she'd ever seen. I didn't do anything but laugh, but now Gabe hates me and keeps threating to hurt me."

Tear-filled eyes looked up at him. "I didn't mean to laugh, but it was funny how mean Gabe had been and Katie just told the truth. I tried to say I was sorry and I didn't mean to hurt his feelings, but that only made him madder. So now, I can't ride because if I do,

Gabe will do something mean to scare my horse so it bucks me off and kills me."

Dramatic, and highly unlikely, but Josh's fear was so great that it didn't matter if it was likely or not.

Isaac thought about his own fear, and how Abigail's loving attention had gotten him through it.

He still hadn't summoned the courage to ride yet, but maybe this was finally the right time.

Isaac squatted to the boy's level. "I know you don't want to go, and I'm not going to make you get on the horse. But I've decided that I'm going to try riding for the first time, and it would mean a lot to me if I had a friend there to support me. Gabe isn't going to do anything to your horse if I'm right there. Let's do this together, and you can show Gabe that you're not afraid of him. And when your parents pick you up, they'll be happy, too."

Josh's eyes widened. "You're really going to do it?"

Isaac nodded. "I'm scared, just like you. But I don't want to be scared anymore. Abigail has helped me make friends with Simba, so maybe it's time for me to actually try to ride him."

Josh looked at him with wonder. "You're really brave."

Isaac nodded. "But I can only be brave if I have a friend there to support me. Will you come and help me? I know I can do it if you're right next to me."

For a moment, Josh hesitated, then he nodded. "I'll be there for you, friend."

Some might think it silly, but having this ten-year-old boy call him *friend* was one of the highest compliments Isaac had ever been given. This lonely little boy, who was struggling to relate to the other children at camp, saw Isaac as a friend.

When they got to the paddock area where the kids were getting ready to ride, he saw that Abigail was still handing out helmets. Though Abigail and her family typically didn't wear helmets when they rode, every child at camp was required to wear one for safety reasons and insurance purposes.

Isaac stopped in front of Abigail. "I'd like a helmet, please," he said.

Abigail reached for the child helmets, probably assuming it was for Josh, but Isaac stopped her.

"No, not for him. For me. I've been afraid to ride horses, but I think it's time I faced my fear. My friend right here, he's gonna watch me and support me."

Josh held out his hand. "So I'll need a helmet too."

An understanding look crossed Abigail's face. It was obvious she knew he was trying to be a good example to the child, but as she handed him the helmet, she leaned in and said, "You don't have to do this, you know."

Isaac took the helmet and put it on his head. "Yes, I do. How can we expect the children to ever overcome their fears, when I'm trapped by the same fear?"

Abigail handed him a lead rope. "I guess you better get Simba, shouldn't you?"

Isaac's hand shook as he took the rope from her, and he knew there would be no shame in backing out. But as he felt Josh's eyes on him, he knew he had to do this. Even though he'd barely begun accepting the idea that there was a God who loved him and wanted to protect them, he couldn't help sending up a little prayer.

Please. Let this be okay.

Abigail gave Josh a rope. "This is for Stretch. He's Simba's best friend, and the two of them prefer to work as a team."

Though Josh still looked terrified, he

smiled. "I like Stretch. I fed him an apple slice the other day."

As they arrived at the stalls, Josh whispered, "It's okay if your stomach hurts. You could go to the infirmary, too."

Isaac shook his head. "No. I'm fine."

The truth was Isaac did feel sick to his stomach. The panic and fear and worry and memories of all of the things that had gone wrong in the past when he tried to ride a horse came flashing back. What if something bad happened and he further traumatized this poor child?

Then from deep within, Isaac felt a strange sense of peace and calm, like God had answered his prayers. Everything was going to be okay. Isaac knew all the safety measures. Over the past couple of weeks, as they taught the kids about horses, Abigail had taught him everything he needed to know to be safe. He mentally rehearsed every step she had told him in going to the stall and catching the horse.

In the past, Isaac hadn't been given the depth of information Abigail had given him. Now, he was ready. He could do this.

Isaac held his hand out to Simba. "Hey, Simbasaur," he said. "I know you know I'm terrified. But I also know that you know I'm your friend. I come out here every day with Abigail and make friends with you. So I need you to be a friend to me today and help me, because I'm scared."

It felt strange, being a grown man, saying these things, but there was a little boy watching. What Josh needed most was to understand that it was okay for a man to be afraid, and it was okay for a man to admit it.

But, also, that he could stand up and face his fears, and he would be better for it.

Isaac looked over at the next stall, where Josh was doing the same thing Isaac had done. He was talking to the horse, admitting his fear, but also telling the horse he trusted him to keep him safe.

They both took their horses and tied them up on the rail where everyone tied up their horses for grooming and saddling, just as Abigail had shown him. When she came over, she smiled. "That's a great knot. Nice job. You too, Josh."

It was weird to swell with pride at such a simple compliment, but he knew Abigail was picky about how people tied the horses because it was important to her that everyone do it safely.

Together, they groomed the horses, and Isaac noted that Josh knew exactly what to do and what to use, and as Isaac encouraged him, all traces of the boy's fear left.

A couple of times, Gabe passed and looked like he was going to say something to Josh, but as soon as he noticed Isaac right next to him, Gabe would back away.

"Just remember our signal," Isaac said. "No matter what makes you feel scared, a horse or Gabe or even something else, I'm here for you."

"Thanks," Josh said.

As they finished saddling the horses, Isaac looked over at Josh's handiwork. "For someone who has never ridden a horse, you sure are an expert."

Josh beamed. "I do know a lot."

Isaac tightened his cinch, then said, "I find that the more I know about something, the less afraid of it I am."

Josh nodded. "It's not so much the saddling as it is the horse after you saddle it. That part you can't control."

Then the boy gestured at the cinch Isaac had just tightened. "He was bloating while you tightened it, so you're going to need to tighten it a bit more."

Isaac hadn't noticed Abigail coming up to them until she laughed. "Yes, Simba has a bad habit of that. Don't you, boy?"

She smiled at Josh. "Great catch. It shows you've been paying attention." Then she reached over and gave Simba a pat.

Simba nuzzled her in response, and once again, Isaac was in awe of the relationship between the woman and the horse. She was the embodiment of the point he had just been trying to prove to Josh. The more familiar you are with something, the less you have to be afraid of it.

Wasn't that what he had learned about Abigail? The more he got to know her, the more he realized what an amazing woman she was and how blessed he was to know her. Sometimes he wished he could turn back time to that first day in class, when he saw her dressed like an old-fashioned schoolmarm, sitting stiffly at her desk.

What he thought was her being stuck-up was likely her nervousness at being in a new situation and her excitement at finally getting to go to school. He wondered if some of his bad impressions of other people had come from a similar place of making assumptions.

He retightened the cinch, noticing that he was able to get it a couple notches tighter. When they finished getting the horses ready, Isaac led Simba off the rail and into the arena. Now was the moment of truth.

Just before he entered the arena, Josh came up next to him with his horse. "Here. I have something for you."

He pulled a tiny dinosaur figurine out of his pocket and handed it to Isaac. "He'll help you be brave."

Wow. Isaac had seen Josh holding the tiny dinosaur when he was nervous, and now the little boy was sharing it with him. It was tempting to tell Josh that he didn't need it, but instead, Isaac accepted it as a gift of love and faith from a child.

Abigail must have seen the exchange, because she came up to the other side of him and whispered, "You're amazing."

Isaac didn't know that he'd go that far, but knowing that Abigail was watching so closely and cared so deeply, he wanted to be the amazing man she'd just said he was.

Finally ready to mount, Isaac shook as he put his foot in the stirrup and swung his leg over to the other side of the horse. Logic told him he was perfectly safe and everything would be fine. But as he sat atop the horse, staring out at everything, he felt a mixture of fear, exhilaration and pride.

Next to him, on Stretch, Josh looked just as terrified as Isaac felt. Isaac scratched his nose, hoping the gesture gave the boy comfort, but also feeling good that he, too, could express his emotions. Josh gave him a thumbs-up and scratched his own nose, so Isaac gave him the thumbs-up back.

Abigail came up beside them and gave two thumbs-up. She'd seen the interaction and was showing her support as well.

The grin on Josh's face made it all worthwhile. Sure, the kid was still afraid, but he also had the loving support he needed to face his fear.

Isaac had promised himself he would never ever get on a horse again, and here he was. Just like Josh, he'd needed loving support to find the courage to try, and he was so grateful Abigail had given it to him.

Abigail walked around, making sure the children were all safely on top of their horses.

She paused at Isaac and Josh on her final lap. "You're both doing great. I've never been more proud of anyone in my entire life."

Her compliment was the final piece of strength he needed to sit up just a little bit straighter, mimicking the pose that she had demonstrated to all the riders as being proper form. When she told them to start getting their horses going, Isaac felt a surge of confidence as he gently squeezed the horse's middle and asked him to go.

As Simba moved forward, Isaac remembered the awkward back-and-forth motion that went with riding a horse. However, it only took a few moments to get used to it, and Isaac found himself caught in an easy rhythm. This wasn't so bad. All this time, he'd lived in fear of something terrible happening, yet here he was, riding a horse like it was the most natural thing in the world.

With every step Simba took, Isaac felt safer and safer.

He glanced at Josh, who also seemed to sit up straighter and more confident with every step.

Katie rode up to them. "You look real good riding Simba," she said. "Not a lot of people get to ride Simba because that's Miss Abigail's special horse."

Isaac reached forward and patted the

horse's neck. "I know. I feel very honored that I get to ride him."

He looked over to where Abigail stood, his eyes seeking hers, and he was rewarded with a soft smile. He'd never felt so much gratitude for a human being in his life. Except, of course, for Mr. P.

Katie looked over at Josh. "You're doing great, too. Stretch is a good horse, and he'll take care of you. Even though this is your first time, you look like you've been riding forever. Maybe someday, we can go on a ride to look for dinosaur bones."

The little girl rode next to him for a few moments, then she got bored of just walking, so she kicked her horse to go a little faster. But as soon as she did, Simba's ears pricked up, as if he, too, had Katie's same adventurous spirit.

Simba took off, faster than Isaac had ever been on a horse. Isaac's stomach dropped to the floor.

Abigail must've noticed the terror on his face because she said, "It's okay. Remember what you do if the horse is going a little too fast for you. Tell him to slow down."

Right. Check and release. He did the motion Abigail had demonstrated to them, and sure enough, Simba listened.

"There you go," Abigail said. "You did it. Now let's see if we can get you trotting with everyone else."

Isaac looked over at Josh to make sure this incident hadn't traumatized the boy, but Josh gave him a thumbs-up. He was already trotting, and as Katie had observed earlier, no one would have known he was too terrified to ride.

He kicked the horse again, and Simba immediately returned to that same faster pace.

"That's right," Abigail said. "Just relax into the trot, and you'll be fine."

Trot? He knew that was the next speed up from walking, but it felt like Simba was running. He was glad he'd gotten the horse under control because it would have been embarrassing to have had an issue with trotting.

Something about Abigail's warm, confident voice gave him what he needed to press on. Isaac continued at the trot, going around with all the children and realizing that with each rocking motion of the horse, he settled more and more into the rhythm.

Yes. He could do this.

Not only was Isaac doing it, but Josh was, as well. The little boy who'd been so terrified to ride that he'd had stomachaches all week to avoid getting on a horse was grinning like he was having the time of his life.

By the end of the hour, Isaac had never felt better about being on a horse. In fact, he almost didn't want to get off, and he was looking forward to the next time he'd get to ride.

The euphoric feeling of having ridden a horse was even better than having done some of his greatest motocross jumps. He got the same exhilarating feeling from both—the thrill of danger and having survived it—and while he intellectually knew that everything he'd ever done in motocross was far more dangerous than the simple trot around the arena, riding this horse had meant he had battled his own personal fears and won.

Isaac had remained a prisoner of terror for so long when it came to horses that this seemed like the biggest victory of his life.

When he got off the horse, it felt like he was walking on air. As soon as he stepped out of the arena, Josh brought Stretch up next to him. "Isaac. You did it."

The warmth of this child congratulating him on a job well done was perhaps the greatest gift he'd ever received, other than Josh trusting him enough to also ride. Josh looked at him as if he was a hero, and all Isaac had done was ride a horse.

"That was amazing," Isaac said. "I'm so glad I did it."

Josh grinned. "Me too! I can see why dinosaur hunters use horses to search for dinosaur bones. You can see everything. Still, that was really scary."

"I was terrified," Isaac said. He caught Abigail's eye, and she walked over to them. "It was the most terrifying thing I've ever done in my entire life," Isaac said. "But I remembered all of the things Abigail taught us about being safe and what to do and how to keep from getting hurt, and the other lessons we've been learning here at camp. In every moment it got scary, I thought about how Abigail told us it would be okay."

Isaac closed his eyes as he thought about how the image of Abigail had brought him so much comfort. Though he was trying to make a point to Josh about how having knowledge brought confidence to your ability to do a task, Isaac realized that it wasn't just the knowledge that had made him feel safe. It was Abigail's soothing presence, her kindness, her lack of judgment even when he had been judging her.

The truth was Isaac had felt safe getting on that horse because Abigail made him feel safe.

For Isaac, safety wasn't just about those things. It was about knowing he could trust someone. Except for Mr. P, Isaac had never been able to trust anyone. Of course, he couldn't say that now. He couldn't tell Josh, nor could he tell Abigail those feelings. But he could encourage this little boy.

The kids all surrounded them, chattering about what a great job they'd done. He was supposed to be the instructor, and yet, today the children had taught him. These children were the encouragement he had needed to overcome his fear.

Even Josh, who had been something of an outcast because of his unwillingness to ride, had gained his admirers. Isaac looked around for Gabe but didn't see the boy. Hopefully, this would be an end to the bullying, but just in case, Isaac would be looking out.

After all the kids had congratulated them, Abigail said, "All right everyone, I know we are very excited for these two, but now we need to put the horses away."

As the children scattered, Isaac noticed Katie had gone up to Josh and said something to him that made him smile, and he went with her and her horse. Maybe that's what this little boy needed as well. Friendship instead of judgment.

Abigail hung back. "What you did was really amazing," she said. "I don't want to make you feel uncomfortable, but you have to know that what you gave those children was an incredible gift. You gave them an example of trying hard things and succeeding. I know that we all questioned whether or not this was the place for you this summer, but what you did for those children today will last a lifetime."

Her words humbled him because even though he had been thinking something similar, it felt odd to hear it from someone he had been judging so harshly.

"I didn't do it for them," he said. "I didn't even think of them until I got done and they were all congratulating me. I just knew that I had to do this for me, and I'm glad that it helped these kids."

The warm smile she gave him put butterflies in his stomach unlike any he had ever known. It felt like the kind of stuff you saw on television that you kind of wanted to gag at because it was just a little too sweet. But having experienced the feeling for the first time in his life, suddenly he understood the appeal of that as well.

"Still, it was very brave, and you didn't have to do it in front of these children," she said. "You could have asked us privately, and we would've done it. I know everyone here has offered to help you many times. But doing it this way meant so much more to everyone."

She leaned in and gave him a warm hug. As he was enveloped by her arms, and he felt the peace wash over him, he couldn't think of any other place he'd rather be.

He could've stayed in her arms forever, but the longer she held him, the more he realized that she was just giving him the same hug she gave every other camper and that the feelings he was having for her were not appropriate given the circumstances.

He pulled away and said, "Thank you. Your support has meant a lot to me. I couldn't have done any of this without you."

The sound of laughter on the other side of the barn drew his attention. Josh and Katie had just finished putting away their tack and were laughing at something.

It was a good reminder of why else he'd made the choice to ride today.

Isaac paused. "And I did it for Josh. Apparently, Gabe has been threatening him, and that was making his fear worse. I needed to be there for him."

"Gabe?" A concerned look flitted onto Abigail's face. "I thought I'd noticed some tension between them, but when I asked Josh about it, he told me that everything was fine. I should have known to dig deeper."

"Let's not make a big deal of it for now. Josh didn't want anyone to know, so let's see if him riding resolves the issue. Apparently, this all started because Josh laughed when Katie called Gabe out because Gabe had been bragging about his riding skills, then had a bad ride."

Abigail nodded. "I remember that. Gabe's pride was really hurt. It doesn't excuse his behavior, but we could all do with another talk about compassion."

Compassion. Something Abigail had in spades, and Isaac appreciated that she always turned to a compassionate approach rather than a retributive one. That was all he'd known his whole life, and he was grateful to see someone else who came from that background choosing to do it differently.

Such a remarkable woman. Sometimes he wished—

A child ran up to them with a question for Abigail, and Isaac was glad for it. It prevented him from finishing what would have been an inappropriate thought. Isaac felt awkward, knowing he was starting to have feelings for Abigail, knowing that they probably weren't appropriate. Okay no probably—definitely. They were coworkers, colleagues and barely friends. At the end of the summer, he would be leaving for Camp Guffey, and she belonged here, with her family.

Why bother starting something neither of them could finish?

A tiny voice in the back of his head said that maybe he should ask her. Let her make that decision for herself. But just as quickly as the thought came, he pushed it aside and reminded himself that romance was not on the menu for him. He had other goals in life, and frankly, having been through the childhood he had, he wasn't sure he had it in him to give what a woman wanted or needed.

Sometimes, he still had nightmares of the sounds of his father beating his mother. It was strange because even though his father had abused him as well, Isaac didn't remember it as clearly. But the sounds of his mother crying and his father's harsh tone of voice would follow him forever.

One time, Isaac suggested to his mother that they run away, as only a small child could, not really understanding what it meant, but his mother had told him that she loved his father, and that he needed them, and that they just had to be understanding and compassionate, and things would get better.

Suddenly, because Abigail's laugh broke through his thoughts, he now understood why he resisted Abigail so much. All his life, he had believed that his mother's idea of loving his father and giving him kindness and love as a response to being beaten was a terrible way of dealing with abuse. All these years, he thought that the whole idea of using love and kindness to change a person was a bunch of nonsense and misguided. Which, in his family's case, was absolutely true. However, Abigail had shown him that there was a difference between giving kindness while tolerating abuse and setting appropriate boundaries while still being compassionate. He'd made fun of Abigail for being naive, but now he had to wonder if perhaps it had been him who was wrong all along.

Isaac had made the judgment that using kindness and love was being weak because his father yelled over and over that Isaac's mother was weak. But maybe using his father's words as a guide for what weakness was and wasn't hadn't been the best idea.

Had he, as a child, actually understood the dynamics between his parents and their abusive relationship?

He knew from his classes that the ideas people get about right and wrong in the world develop as children. While they shape who people are as adults, the ideas are often inaccurate, especially when the child comes from an abusive home.

Sometimes the biggest lesson people have to learn as adults is how to unravel those inaccuracies and instead see the truth. Isaac thought he'd done that, but Abigail's love and kindness had given him a deeper understanding. It had given him the strength and courage to do something incredibly difficult.

This realization should have made him feel better and made him want to think about pursuing Abigail. But instead it made him realize just how deep some of his childhood wounds were. He didn't know what was going to come up, and he couldn't risk hurting such a wonderful woman.

As he put away his tack, he reminded himself that as much as Abigail and her love had helped him, it was only for the summer.

She shouldn't have hugged him like that. Abigail chided herself for the momentary lapse in judgment that had made her hug Isaac. Sure, it was normal for her to hug people, especially during a moment of pride or happiness.

But this was different. Hugging Isaac was different.

Even though they'd been working out in the hot sun with kids all day, she had breathed in his scent greedily, wanting as much as she could take in. By the time Isaac pulled away, Abigail had realized that this wasn't a friend hug, at least not for her.

Had he realized it? Had he sensed her more than friendly feelings toward him? It had been easy to ignore the crush she'd had on him when she thought he was a jerk. She'd been able to pretend that she felt nothing for him because she hadn't seen him in such an admirable light. But when you saw someone face an incredible fear and overcome it, you couldn't look at them the same way anymore.

She certainly didn't see Isaac unfavorably. It was hard to even imagine why she disliked him in the first place. Yes, she hated his tough-guy attitude. But now she saw the vulnerability underneath. After the night when they talked about forgiveness and faith, Abigail felt a new closeness to him, and she understood him on a deeper level.

How could he understand things like forgiveness and love when he'd never experienced it? It was true that Maddie had hurt them all, but if it hadn't been for Maddie's lies, they wouldn't have Kayla in their lives, and Kayla was one of the brightest spots in their family. Her smile, her laughter, all the joy she brought to them—all that would have been lost. Lives had been touched through Kayla, and Abigail had to believe that as with Joseph in the Bible, whose brothers had meant him harm, God had planned all of those bad things for the good, the saving of many lives. Just like Joseph had forgiven his brothers, they too had to forgive Maddie.

Hopefully, the love they continued to

share as a family would be an example to Isaac, and he would continue to grow in his faith.

Yes, that was it.

Rather than focusing on her personal feelings for Isaac, Abigail had to continue focusing on helping him and building him up, just as she did for everyone else.

Abigail focused on the more important task at hand, working with the children. As she supervised them putting away the last of the tack, she forced herself to put Isaac out of her mind. Her focus had to be on the children. Even though a secret part of her had always wished she could find a love of her own, the truth was she was so busy taking care of the kids in the stables that she didn't have room for anything else in her life.

The few times she'd been interested in someone, the potential relationship had been too distracting, and her feelings weren't strong enough for her to pursue it. What mattered was the stables and the work they were doing for the children. Her own personal happiness didn't matter in the context of the larger mission.

Though part of herself tried to call her out for being a liar, Abigail pushed it aside. Even if she decided to take a chance and pursue a romantic relationship for herself, all the reasons she'd given Josie for not wanting to pursue a relationship with Isaac were still valid.

Isaac was a good man, and though she wished she could have something more with him, especially in light of his vulnerability and desire to grow, it wasn't fair to either of them to think of him in this way. She'd do what she could to keep her distance and protect her heart.

Chapter Eight

Keeping her promise to put distance between herself and Isaac was much harder than Abigail had anticipated. A few days later, she watched as Isaac threw a football to a couple of boys as they prepared the children to leave. The way he smiled and joked with them brought a lightness to her heart. He genuinely loved the kids, and part of her wished he could stay.

But she knew that was impossible, and she wouldn't even ask.

And despite her desire to stop thinking about her silly crush on him, she couldn't help but find his laugh as he failed to catch the football the most attractive thing ever.

Trying to push that thought out of her head, Abigail turned her attention to Katie and Josh huddled over a book. It was good to see the two children bonding. Because Josh was homeschooled, he didn't know any of the local kids from school, and from what Abigail had learned, a lot of the kids at school picked on Katie. Maybe that was why she'd always had a soft spot for the child.

Abigail noticed Gabe, the boy Isaac had mentioned to her, walking over to Josh and Katie. As Abigail took a step toward them to make sure everything would be all right, Gabe knocked the book out of Josh's hands, and it fell into a mud pile.

Abigail got there just as Gabe said, "Oops, sorry," in a way that indicated Gabe was anything but.

"That didn't look like an accident to me," Abigail said.

Katie had already picked up the book and was frantically wiping at it. "My dad and I got this when we were on one of his trips," Katie, said crying. "It's a special book, and you can't get it just anywhere."

Isaac had also noticed the drama between the children and had walked over. He held his hand out to Katie. "Do you mind if I take a look? I'm kind of an expert at fixing books that have been dropped in the mud."

Katie sniffled and looked up at him, wide-eyed. "You don't think it's ruined?"

Isaac smiled and held his hand out to her. "I'm pretty sure I can fix it."

Just as they started to walk off, Katie's stepmother pulled up, honking the horn frantically. She was always in a hurry to pick Katie up, so Abigail knew Katie wouldn't be able to wait for Isaac to fix the book. Isaac seemed to sense the same thing.

"Is it okay if I keep your book overnight?" he asked. "I'll do my best to have it as good as new for you in the morning."

Katie looked nervously at the car that was waiting for her, and she nodded. "Okay. If you think you can fix it."

She ran toward the car, then stopped, turned around and waved at Josh. "Bye, Josh. See you tomorrow."

The way the little girl's face lit up when she said goodbye to Josh made Abigail smile. She was grateful they'd found friends in one another.

Which left something else to deal with. Abigail turned to Gabe. "You're on lunch cleanup duty for the rest of the week," she said. "You need to learn to respect other people's property."

Gabe glared at her. "I said it was an accident."

This wasn't the first bully Abigail had dealt with, and it certainly wouldn't be the last, but it was funny that they all thought they had the upper hand. "I saw it happen. If the book can't be fixed, I will be talking to your parents about you providing a replacement for Katie. She loves that book, and what you did wasn't right."

Gabe glared at her, a defiant look in his eyes. "You can try, but my dad will believe me when I say it was an accident, and you won't get a penny out of him. He's a lawyer."

The boy turned and pointed at a car that had just pulled up. "And there's my dad now. Bye."

He walked off as if he hadn't been in trouble. This was Gabe's first summer at the camp, and his family was new to town, so Abigail didn't know them well. She'd have to spend a little more time getting to know them so that she could understand better why Gabe behaved the way he did. Abigail didn't know why he picked on Josh and Katie, but Abigail would keep an eye on them all to see if she could figure out the dynamic.

The rest of the kids were picked up, and

Abigail went back into the barn to see where Isaac had gone to fix the book. He was in the staff kitchen, carefully wiping the mud off of it.

"How bad is it?" she asked.

Isaac shook his head. "Not bad at all. I'm just taking a lot of care to make sure that what I'm using to clean it doesn't cause more damage. It won't be as good as new, but the untrained eye would never know anything happened to it."

Who would've thought that some burly man who rode a motorcycle would take such tender care in repairing a child's damaged book? That was the thing about Isaac. Nothing about him was as it seemed, and the more she got to know him, the more she liked him.

It warmed her heart to see how well he cared for all the children, but the image she couldn't get out of her mind was the terrified man bravely getting on the horse.

If only they weren't in such different places in their lives, she could see herself falling for him.

"What you did the other day was amazing," she said.

Isaac carefully set the book aside and

turned to look at her. "It's what anyone would do. This book means something to Katie, so of course I'm going to do whatever I can to make it better."

"I didn't mean that," she said. "I meant riding Simba."

For a moment, Isaac looked like a bashful schoolboy. "It was something I had to do. If don't you face the things you're afraid of, how will you ever overcome your fears? I don't want to be afraid of riding, so the only way to conquer it is to do it."

"We've tried for three years to get Josh to ride," Abigail said. "You inspired him."

Isaac shrugged. "He inspires me. The poor kid doesn't want to be here, doesn't feel like he fits in, and I know what that's like. And yet, he still comes every day and faces bullies like that Gabe kid. He's just trying to do the best he can to get through. I lived that life, so I get him."

It was one of the many things she admired about Isaac. He didn't see what he did as being extraordinary. He just saw himself as a person who recognized someone going through what he had, wanting to help them through it. In class, she'd pegged him as an egotistical jerk who thought he was better than everyone else. Now she could see that he was just someone who had been there and was sharing from the perspective of having lived it rather than following a textbook.

Further evidence of how they were more alike than different. Abigail's whole reason for investing in all of these children was so that they had the positive light in their lives that she hadn't had. So funny that two people who were so different could have so much in common.

Maybe it was foolish, but even though she'd technically run out of camp-related things to discuss, Abigail didn't want to end the conversation. She enjoyed being in Isaac's company and didn't want their time together to end.

"I was going to go for a walk to stretch my legs and clear my mind. If you wanted to come," she said. She didn't know where that offer had come from, though she did take a walk every afternoon after class got out. It was her way of clearing away the day before she jumped into all the family things she had to do.

Isaac smiled at her. "I've seen you out walking. I was wondering where the trail or something was because I often like to walk to clear my head, so I'd like that."

She pushed aside the voice that pointed out that this was one more thing they had in common. She didn't need those reminders. It was hard enough riding the line between being friends and wishing for something that could never be.

"There isn't one. At least not for another quarter mile or so down the road. But I have this little route that I take around the property that's my way of shifting gears for the day. I'm happy to show it to you."

Once they got out of the stables area and to the fence line she liked to walk, Abigail felt the stress of the day leaving her. Usually she relished this time to be alone, but there was something extremely comforting about having Isaac by her side.

If only things could be different. He'd already shown her what an amazing man he was in all the little things. As much as she'd tried to not like him and to remind herself of all the things she'd told Josie about why she couldn't be with him, after seeing him ride Simba and the tender way he'd taken care of Katie's book, it was becoming harder and harder to accept the reasons she'd given her cousin.

As they passed her favorite spot to think, Isaac paused. "This is a great rock," he said. "It reminds me of a place I used to go to at Camp Guffey that was away from all the noise and activity and just gave me some space to relax."

Abigail smiled at him. "It's funny you say that. This is where I like to go to think."

"I'm not surprised at all," Isaac said. "The more time I spend with you, the more I realize how much alike we are. Sometimes I think you're my other half, which is silly, but it's like you're a part of me I didn't know I was missing."

The tenderness in his eyes as he spoke drew her to him. "I'm not sure I would describe it the same way," she said. "But I do find myself thinking that you've so quickly become a part of my life, and I don't want to see you go."

Isaac took her hands in his. "They may not be the same words, but I think they mean the same thing. There's something special between us, and I know this is unprofessional since we're technically working together, but I would be a fool if I didn't take the opportunity to let you know that I have feelings for you."

The warmth of her hands in his brought an unexpected thrill to Abigail. No one had ever spoken to her like that, and she certainly never expected those words from him. As much as she loved the feeling, and wished she could embrace it, there were too many other things to consider. Reasons why this shouldn't happen.

"But I'm so much older than you," she said. "I could almost be your mother."

Isaac laughed. "Almost, but not quite. I did the math."

He did the math? If Isaac had gone so far as to calculate the difference in their ages and the appropriateness of their relationship, then he must have been thinking about this for a while.

Abigail pulled her hands from his. "That doesn't bother you?"

Isaac shrugged. "I mean, I thought about it, but no. Age is just a number. I've always been a believer that we care for who we care for, and I care for you. I don't look at you and see the number of your age. I see a remarkable woman standing before me with an incredibly giving heart. And I want to win that heart."

He leaned forward and pressed his lips to hers gently. The soft brush of his lips brought a wave of happiness to her unlike anything she'd ever known. But as he tried to deepen the kiss, she couldn't get her brain to stop thinking of all the reasons why they didn't belong together.

Sure, he said right now that he didn't mind their age difference, but he was in the throes of infatuation, not trying to build a life with her. As she pulled away, she thought again about all the reasons she couldn't get involved with Isaac. Even though he'd agreed to go to church with them on Sunday, it didn't mean they were a spiritual match. His idealistic views of what their relationship could be hadn't faced the reality of a younger man being with an older woman. Plus, there was still the fact that he was leaving at the end of the summer.

As beautiful as the kiss had been, it would lead to nothing but heartache for them both.

"That shouldn't have happened," Abigail said.

Isaac looked distraught. "Did I misread the signs? Did I make an unwelcome pass?"

Abigail shook her head, hating that she'd made him feel bad. "No. I wanted that kiss just as much as you, but I got to thinking just how impractical it is for us to pursue this."

The disappointed look on his face made

her heart hurt, so she added, "You're leaving at the end of the summer, and my place is here. Is it right for us to pursue something, when in the end, we know we can't build anything?"

Isaac nodded slowly. "To be honest, it's why I haven't spoken of my feelings sooner. I've tried to ignore how I feel about you, but it's hard because you're such a wonderful woman."

Abigail smiled at him, wishing it wasn't so hard, but grateful they understood each other. Though they both admitted to having feelings for each other, they were also smart enough to recognize the danger to their hearts before either of them got hurt.

"I feel the same way about you. But it's wrong for us to pursue a romance when we know it's never going anywhere."

Isaac nodded. "I don't want to admit it, but you're right. I've never been one for casual relationships. Even if I was, you deserve better than that."

They walked back to the stables in silence, a new tension between them that made Abigail wish she hadn't invited Isaac on the walk to begin with.

If this is what heartbreak felt like, Abigail was glad she'd never done much in the dating world. The lump that formed in her throat stayed with her until they got back to the stables and went their separate ways.

Even then, Abigail couldn't escape the feeling in the pit of her stomach. She went into her office, and the first thing she noticed was the vision board taped to her wall, with all the places she wanted to travel. It felt like a waste of time dreaming about all these places that she could never visit because the stables needed her too much.

Just like with the momentary thought that she might be able to find love for herself. What a joke.

Yes, it had felt wonderful to receive Isaac's admission that he had feelings for her. But it also felt terrible knowing that it wasn't meant to be.

Why did Abigail waste her time thinking about things she could never have?

Ouch. This was why Isaac didn't put himself out there with women. Kissing Abigail had been a risk, but it had felt so right in the moment that he'd failed to consider the implications.

Abigail was a kind, loving woman with

a big heart. Which was exactly why he was attracted to her.

Yes, he understood her reasons, and to tell the truth, he agreed. He couldn't believe he'd been so weak as to kiss her, knowing that this relationship couldn't go anywhere. It wasn't fair to either of them.

It hurt, knowing that as much as he wanted this relationship, as much as he loved being part of this family, it wasn't possible. He had to console himself with the knowledge that he had a far greater mission, as did Abigail.

That was what Abigail had done her whole life, and as hard as it was to accept, he knew this was for the best. Everyone in her family thought her sacrifice in giving up her dreams to raise her sister and cousin was so great. But Isaac understood. Love for others was far greater than one's personal happiness.

Maybe some were fortunate enough to get both. But if they didn't, it was enough to know that they were making a difference in the world in their own way.

So why did this make his heart hurt so much?

As he looked around the property, he wished he could be the guy willing to give up his dream of Camp Guffey. As much as he loved working with the kids here, his heart was all about helping the children in foster care. His own bad experiences, combined with seeing the way Abigail and her family loved others, had made him even more passionate in his desire to be the love for these kids.

And yet, Abigail was right. How could they combine their shared passion with different life directions?

Still, as he walked past Simba's stall on his way back to his quarters, he couldn't help remembering the way they'd connected over this silly horse.

He paused at the horse.

"What am I supposed to do here?"

A few weeks ago, if you'd told him that he'd be talking to a horse like a friend, he'd have laughed in your face. But now, he could understand how Abigail had said that he was her best friend. You could tell Simba whatever you wanted, and he didn't judge you. He just listened.

And then, Isaac thought about what Abigail had said to him about God. Though talking to a horse definitely felt good, Isaac could talk to God. Simba couldn't give him the answers he needed, but as Isaac turned his attention to God, he prayed that God would help him see the way to solutions to his dilemma.

Letting Abigail go was what he should do. But even as he prayed, he didn't feel peace about that decision. But what else was he supposed to do?

Chapter Nine

Though Isaac knew that God wasn't in the business of answering prayers on demand or on anyone's personal schedule, it was frustrating that in the days that followed his ill-timed kiss with Abigail, Isaac felt even more distanced from her. His head kept telling him that space was what they both needed, but his heart longed to reconnect with her. He was supposed to be supervising the children for pickup, but he found himself too distracted with his thoughts of Abigail. At least until he heard Katie yell, "Stop it, you big bully."

He turned to look, and once again, Gabe had taken her book. Isaac was pleased to note that this time, it wasn't a dinosaur book, but instead, she'd been showing Josh a horse book. This was the first time he'd seen the boy show any interest in the horse information, and he smiled because he realized that this was the sort of thing people did when they cared about someone else.

He stole a glance at Abigail, who had her back to them as she was helping some other children.

He went over to where the children were arguing. "What's going on over here?" he asked.

Katie pointed at Gabe. "He took my book and won't give it back."

Isaac had successfully repaired the other book Gabe had tried to destroy, so hopefully, the boy wouldn't damage this one.

"Gabe, that book doesn't belong to you, so give it back to Katie."

Even though Gabe was still much shorter than Isaac, he held the book above his head. "I just wanted to look at it," he said.

Isaac stared at the boy. "You can't look at it with it above your head," he said. "And besides that, it's Katie's book, and it doesn't seem like she wants you to have it."

Gabe glared at Katie. "She's just a dumb girl, so I don't have to listen to her," he said.

"We don't talk about girls in that way,"

Isaac said. "We don't talk like that about anyone, so you need to apologize."

Gabe still held the book, and Isaac didn't want to antagonize him so much that the boy did something retaliatory like damage Katie's book. But this behavior also couldn't be tolerated.

Abigail must have noticed what was going on because she joined them. "What's going on here?"

"Gabe stole Katie's book and won't give it back, and he's also saying unkind things about Katie."

Abigail stared at Gabe. "Gabe, we talked about this. Why are you still being unkind to Katie? Didn't you learn your lesson from lunch duty?"

Gabe glared at her. "You're just a stupid girl, too," Gabe said. "And my dad says that girls are useless except for having babies. I don't even know why they let a dumb girl be in charge."

"Enough," Isaac said. "We don't talk about women that way."

He didn't realize he'd actually been yelling at the boy until he stopped and saw the shocked expressions on everyone's faces around him. The worst was the look of utter disappointment on Abigail's face. She looked at him like he was a stranger, and perhaps he was, because even he didn't recognize the man who had spoken so harshly to a child.

Gabe shrank back, like he was terrified of Isaac, and Isaac felt an even deeper level of shame. He had never wanted to make a child fear him, and had never imagined that he could be someone who would make a child feel so scared. Yet here he was, just like his father.

"I'm sorry, sir," Gabe said, his voice shaking. "It won't happen again."

Rather than making him feel better, the boy's apology only made Isaac feel worse. How many times had he, because he was terrified, given that same apology he didn't mean? Gabe was only saying what he needed to say to placate the man who had just yelled at him so he wouldn't be hit.

Gabe wouldn't try to do better in how he treated women because he'd realized it was wrong; he was just trying to keep Isaac from losing his temper further. Isaac gave the boy a nod, even though right now, he wanted to run away and throw up in the bushes. He'd done everything he could to not become his father, and now look at him.

Yet, despite the realization that he was a monster, Isaac had to remain where he was and do his best to hold it together.

"Thank you," Isaac said. "Now give Katie her book back."

Gabe handed it to Katie, saying, "I'm sorry for taking your book."

Once a semblance of order was restored, Isaac turned to Abigail. "I need a moment to collect myself. Will you be okay handling the remainder of the pickup?"

Isaac tried not to sprint on his way to the barn. He didn't even know where he was going until he ended up at Simba's stall.

"Simba," he said. "I messed up real bad. All my life, I've been trying not to be like my father. I didn't want to make people feel afraid or like they didn't matter. I never wanted people to respond to me out of fear. But I did it. I acted just like him."

"No, you didn't," Abigail said.

Isaac turned to look at her, wishing she didn't have such a kind and forgiving expression on her face.

"You support me?" he asked. "You heard how I treated that boy."

"A boy who was tormenting a little girl and making incredibly rude and sexist remarks," Abigail said. "Sure, you raised your voice, but you didn't hurt him."

"I could have," he said.

"Did you want to?"

Isaac shook his head. "No. Of course not. But in that moment, my anger replaced all rational thought. What if I had hurt that child? I saw the fear in his eyes. I never imagined I could cause that in anyone."

Isaac leaned against the stall door. "I hate my father," he said. "My whole life, I sought to run away from the monster. I did everything I could to not be like him. But here I am."

Abigail put her arm around him. "You're not a monster. You're a man who got caught up in a moment of frustration, but you never acted on that frustration. You didn't cause him any harm."

He brushed her arm off him, hating the tender look she gave him. Didn't she realize what a monster he was? As much as her rejection of him had stung, looking at it now, he was grateful they hadn't pursued a romantic relationship. What might he do to this woman he cared deeply about in a moment of anger?

Still, Abigail gave him a look of compassion he didn't deserve. "As for you hating him, I encourage you to think about what it would be like to forgive him instead. You've been moved by the things that we've had to forgive in our family. Maybe, it's time you looked at what your father did to you, and instead of being driven by the hate you have for him, think about the fact that God loves him. Take the time to forgive him, let go of the pain and let God deal with him."

Isaac had heard similar words from others before, but Abigail didn't know all the things he'd been through, all the ways his father had hurt him and had hurt others.

"Do you know why I struggle with the idea of faith?" Isaac asked. "My father supposedly found Jesus one of the times he was in jail, but when he got out, he came all the way to Minnesota, searching for me at Camp Guffey, and in trying to kidnap me to make us a family again, he burned down the caretaker's cottage, killing the caretaker. He says he's repented of that sin, too, but none of that repentance can undo what he's done. It's why I always return his letters to him unopened. I spent too many years listening to his apologies, believing in his promises, only to turn around and have him hurt me again."

Abigail looked at him with such compassion that he wished he could be the man she seemed to think he could be. "Forgiveness isn't about letting your father off the hook. It's not about saying what he did was right. It's about letting go of the things you hold against him, so that you can be free. As long as you're clinging to your hate, you're clinging to him. We will never be free of him until you let go."

Let go? Easier said than done. And he didn't know how to let go. That didn't even seem like a rational idea. Let go. He wasn't clinging to his father, but he was doing his best to do exactly the opposite.

Isaac shook his head. "That may be true, at least for some people. But you have no idea what my father has done."

He hated the look of disappointment that Abigail gave him. Even though they'd agreed that there couldn't be anything between them romantically, Isaac still hated the thought of disappointing her. He wanted to live up to the man she seemed to think he could be, even though he thought her faith in him was misplaced.

"No, I don't. But you've given me some idea, and I'm not saying it's easy. I just know that the burden of carrying this pain is heavy, and you deserve better."

She hesitated, then said, "God wants better for you. You didn't believe that the love we showed Maddie was possible for anyone, and now you've seen that love in action. Maybe you should give forgiveness a try."

How did you tell someone who meant well thanks, but no thanks? Especially someone he cared for as much as Abigail.

She gave him a soft smile, like she understood the turmoil in his heart. "I know you probably need some time alone, so I'm going to leave. But if you want to talk or just need me to sit with you, I'm here."

She paused at the doorway as she left. "I really do hope that you spend some time talking to God about your father and consider what it might look like to forgive him. You deserve to be free, and you're never going to be as long as you carry around this hatred."

As she left, he could feel the anger welling up in him. She couldn't possibly understand how this felt. She didn't know what he'd been through.

The sound of someone coming into the other end of the barn caught his attention, and the last thing Isaac wanted was to have to talk to anyone else or have someone else tell him that he needed to forgive his father.

He couldn't remember the last time he'd felt so angry and disappointed in himself.

As he turned to leave the barn, he spied a bale of hay. Not knowing what came over him or why, he turned and kicked it with all of his might.

In that instant, Isaac was disgusted with himself. He had never lashed out in anger like this before. How could he have done this?

Sure, he knew that Abigail would tell him that it didn't count because he'd taken his anger out on the hay bale, not a human, but that was what Abigail didn't understand about him. He'd always worked so hard to keep his temper and anger in check and losing control like this was everything he tried not to do.

What, then, was he supposed to do? All he could think about was Abigail's advice to pray. At this point, he didn't have any other options. He couldn't be his father.

As he walked to the thinking rock Abigail had shown him, a text buzzed on his phone from Mr. P.

Maybe Mr. P would give him the clarity he needed.

However, when he read the text, his heart shattered.

Your father was taken to the prison hospital. Only days to live. You need to make peace with him. Call me.

Isaac had long been frustrated that Mr. P had chosen to have a relationship with his father and correspond with him in prison after everything his father had done to cause harm. But Mr. P had always told him that holding a grudge was like giving yourself poison and hoping your enemy would die. Though Mr. P had never talked about forgiveness in the context of God, Isaac realized that all the things Mr. P had told him over the years about letting go of his hatred of his father were exactly the same as what Abigail had been saying about forgiveness.

Okay, fine. Message received. Though he didn't like it, he knew that God kept leading him to the same place.

But did Isaac truly have the strength to forgive his father? To make peace with him before it was too late?

As he took a deep breath and said a gut-wrenching prayer that God would give him what he needed to make it happen, he knew that the only way he'd make it through was if he had Abigail by his side.

But leaning on her for something so important and not falling deeper in love with her seemed even more impossible than forgiving his father.

Abigail spotted Isaac in the distance, walking toward the thinking rock. Part of her wanted to go to him, to continue their conversation about letting go of his hatred of his father. But she already felt like she'd overstepped, and she'd seen the way he'd kicked that bale of hay.

No, she didn't think him a violent man, or anything like his father. But he needed to work through this himself. Or at least accept her offer of help.

Though maybe it was for the best. Abigail desperately wanted to be there for him. She'd seen how her sister and cousin had partners to help them work through their issues, and she wanted the same for herself. More importantly, she wanted it for Isaac.

But as she thought of Isaac allowing some other woman in his life to help him with this, Abigail's heart hurt. *She* wanted to be the woman helping him.

Why had she kissed him?

She'd asked herself that every day since

the kiss, and now, watching him deal with his pain alone was the hardest thing she'd ever done.

A text message buzzed on her phone, and she glanced at it. Kori Anderson—now Bishop—sharing a picture from the wedding on the beach in Costa Rica that she'd missed. An ache filled Abigail's heart.

What would it be like to stand barefoot in the sand with the man you loved?

At this point, she didn't even know how she'd ever get to stand barefoot in the sand, let alone with a man she loved.

But as laughter rang out from the yard, where Kayla was chasing the twins, Abigail reminded herself that some sacrifices were worth it.

She might not have romantic love in her life, but there were other kinds of love, and they were just as fulfilling.

Still, she couldn't find the lightness in her heart that usually came from watching the kids.

This was the life she'd chosen, though, so Abigail started toward the yard. As she did so, Isaac walked up to her. Strange, since she'd just seen him going to the thinking rock.

"I need your help," he said. "My father is

in the hospital, dying. He's been in prison in Minnesota, and Mr. P has stayed in touch with him, so Mr. P called me. I don't know what to do."

The anguish on his face nearly tore her heart in two.

Here she was, feeling bad about personal issues that seemed shallow in comparison to what Isaac was going through, and he was dealing with real trauma. What was wrong with her?

Abigail took a deep breath and held out her hand. "Let's go inside and get my family together. We'll help you figure it out."

As he took her hand, the pain in her heart lessened. This was why she made the sacrifices she had. Family was everything, and if they worked together, they could solve anything. They needed each other, and everything Abigail gave up for the benefit of her family was worth it.

Someday, she hoped Isaac could see that for himself as well.

Chapter Ten

As Abigail sat in the kitchen with her family and Isaac, discussing the text and ensuing phone call he had received from Mr. P about his father being on his deathbed, all she wanted to do was hold him in her arms and tell him it was going to be okay. But they'd already crossed too many lines in the relationship, which left her sitting there, twisting her hands with nothing to do.

"I think you should go," Brady said.

Josie nodded. "I agree. My biggest regret with my father is that I didn't come all the times Abigail tried to get me to make peace with him. Since he died suddenly, I never got the chance to visit him on his deathbed."

She looked down. "I still wouldn't have come, and I think I would have regretted that even more."

Abigail's arguments with Josie over making peace with her father had been some of the most painful things they'd had to deal with. Though they'd talked through all of this and repaired their relationship, Abigail had never imagined that the pain they'd been through together could possibly help Isaac.

"I know I often sounded angry with you when you tried to get us to make peace," Josie said. "Looking back, I know it was because you cared. Obviously, no one can make another person do what they don't want to do. Ultimately, it's their choice."

Josie turned her attention to Isaac. "I know you're not exactly part of our family, but we still care for you as though you were. And we will love and respect you no matter what."

The look on his face when Josie called him *family* nearly broke Abigail's heart. How long had he waited for a connection to family? And even though she agreed with Josie's sentiment, it hurt knowing that he could never be at the level of family Abigail wished he could be.

"I don't know if I can do this alone," Isaac said.

"Why doesn't Abigail go with you?" Josie

asked, looking at her. "It's clear you trust her, and there's nobody I would rather have by my side during a difficult time."

Abigail stared at Josie. Did she just get voluntold to go with Isaac to visit his dying father?

Her immediate response of shock was replaced with a deep longing. The truth was she did want to go. She wanted to be there by his side and hold his hand and help him through all of these difficult emotions.

No one had ever been there for Isaac, and this was her chance to give that to him.

She let out a long sigh. But it was impossible.

"I can't," she said.

Abigail looked at Isaac, hoping he could see the compassion and love in her eyes.

"We're in the middle of camp season, and I don't know how we're going to find a replacement for you, let alone me. I hope you know that I wish I could come with all my heart, and I will always be just a phone call away. I promise, no matter what, I will pick up the phone when you call."

Isaac didn't say anything. Instead he just stared at the table, seemingly lost in his own emotions and thoughts.

"I can help," Maddie said. "I have a ton of vacation time that I never use, so I'll just take time off from the nursing home, and I can help with the camp. After everything you've done for me and Kayla, I feel like it's the least I can do."

The sound of laughter came from the other room, where Kayla was entertaining the twins and the babies. It was on the tip of her tongue to tell Maddie that helping one another was what families did, but then Abigail realized that this was exactly what Maddie was trying to do for her.

Still, while Abigail appreciated the gesture, she shook her head. "But you are just one person. I need two people to cover if I go. However, I will accept your offer of help because I don't know how else I will replace Isaac. But I can't go."

As Abigail spoke, her stomach twisted in a knot as she realized how desperately she did want to go. She stole a glance at Isaac to see if he understood that while she wanted to go, she simply couldn't.

Josie looked over at Laura, and Laura nodded like they were having some kind of secret side conversation, then Josie said, "Usually I take a hands-on role in the camp, but since I just had the baby, I've been stuck in the office so that I can have her with me. I will take your place in your class, and Laura can watch the baby for me. There you go. You needed two people to cover camp, and you got them."

Abigail loved that her cousin and sister were willing to make this sacrifice for her. "I can't do that. The point of having you in the office is that you have the special bonding time with your baby."

Then she looked at Laura, noting the weariness in her sister's eyes. "You're taking care of two toddlers and the baby, so how can we throw another baby into the mix? You're exhausted enough as it is."

"Abigail," Brady said in his quiet and no-nonsense way that meant he wasn't going to accept an argument. "Do you want to go or not?"

Abigail swallowed the tears that were threatening. "It's not a simple question."

Isaac pounded his fist on the table. "Enough. It is that simple. We all know what this is about."

He looked at Abigail, his face so unreadable she thought she was staring at a stranger. But then she remembered. This was the man from her classes who she hated. Harsh, judgmental. But now that she knew him deeper, she understood something in this conversation had touched a nerve for him.

"Here's the reality," Isaac said. "Of course Abigail wants to go. But she's afraid of stepping out of her comfort zone and doing anything where she has to let go of control of her carefully constructed world at the stables."

He stared at her, like he was examining something deep within her. "I see you, Abigail. You push everyone to face their fears, to take risks and to do the hard things. But you know what I think?"

He gestured in the direction of the barn where her office was. "I think the truth is, you're scared. You have all those travel pictures out there, and if you said to your family that you wanted to go on one of those trips, they would find a way for you to get away for a week. But whatever it is that you're afraid of, you can't let go."

He shook his head at her, and she didn't realize how much his disappointment hurt. More importantly, it hurt because she knew he was right.

Abigail was scared, and she didn't even know what she was scared of. Tears rolled down her face, and she didn't understand why this all had to be so hard, but when she started crying, she couldn't stop.

Everyone in the room was silent, like they also didn't understand what had happened. Or maybe, they, too, realized the painful truth in Isaac's words.

Her family would help her find a way to travel if she asked. She'd saved up plenty of money, so what was stopping her from doing the things she'd dreamed of?

The Bible says *ye have not because ye ask not*, and the harsh truth that Isaac had just exposed to her was that of all the desires of her heart, most of the ones lost to her were lost simply because she'd never asked.

Then she looked up and saw Isaac's face.

He, too, was crying.

But they weren't the same kind of tears. It was as if something inside him had broken, and she didn't understand where it was coming from.

Didn't he realize the gift he'd just given her?

"What's wrong?" Abigail asked.

"I did it again," he said. "I struck out in anger, only this time it was at someone I care about."

The anguish on his face nearly broke her heart.

"I'm sorry, Abigail. I didn't mean to hurt you. I didn't mean to say harsh things to you. I didn't mean to make you cry. But clearly, you're right. I do need to go see my father and work out whatever this is, and I need to find better ways to manage my emotions and my anger because the last thing I ever wanted was to hurt someone I love."

Did he just say he loved her? Abigail stared at him, unable to believe what she'd just heard.

"No, you didn't hurt me," Abigail said. "You only told the truth."

He shook his head slowly. "I am so, so sorry. This is why I don't do relationships."

Clearly, they both had their own fears to work through. Was it possible that Abigail's unwillingness to pursue anything with him was also about her fears?

She took a deep breath. Of course it was.

Abigail was afraid of so many things, and loving a man like Isaac was at the top of her list.

But that wasn't important now.

What was important was that he was facing one of the biggest challenges of his life, and he needed her, but she was too scared to take the leap and be there for him.

Before she could process that emotion, Isaac looked at her.

"I'm sorry, Abigail," he said, rising. "I don't want you to come with me. I pushed too hard."

Then he looked around at the rest of her family, who'd assembled in the kitchen specifically to help him figure out what to do, and said, "Thank you all for your help. I'll do my best to be back for next week's classes. But I think it's best if I keep my distance for the rest of the summer."

Wyatt shot him a glare. "You sit right back down. You're family, and we don't let family go through this kind of thing alone. You will not keep your distance, and whatever this is, we will work through it."

Her brother-in-law's words reminded Abigail of the strength they all had when they worked together. Just as she'd been trying to do it all alone, Isaac was, too, and neither of them had to.

Isaac shook his head slowly as he looked at Abigail. "You see that?" he asked, gesturing at her. "Look at what I did to her. She can't stop crying because of how cruel I was."

Abigail reached for a napkin and blew her nose. "You weren't cruel. You told the truth."

She looked around her at family, seeing the love and concern on their faces and realizing that as hard as Isaac's words had been to hear, the deeper truth God had been showing her in this conversation was important for her to face.

"I am afraid. I've had to maintain such tight control over everything that happens here for as long as I can remember that I am terrified that if I let go for just one instant, everything is going to fall apart."

As the words came out, she felt a burden lift from her. She hadn't realized how she'd been feeling until now, but it all made sense.

"I will go with you," Abigail said. "Not because I think I have to, but because I want to. I want to be there with you to help you through this. I don't think I could even be effective here at the camp, knowing you were there going through all of this alone."

Isaac hadn't sat back down yet, but she could see him wavering. He saw the woman who was terrified of letting go of control because it seemed like every time she loosened her grip just a little bit, things fell apart. He'd seen it all along, and he'd been encouraging her to let others help, but she hadn't allowed herself to accept it.

As she looked back at every seemingly bad thing that had happened at the stables, she realized how much she blamed herself every time something went wrong. Like when Josie left, Abigail hadn't been there for the fight Josie had had with Uncle Joe. Part of Abigail had thought that if she hadn't gone out to the movies that night with her friends, she would have been able to defuse the situation like she always had, and Josie would've stayed. However, in hindsight, she could see how that had been a stupid thought because all Josie wanted was to go to college, and Uncle Joe would have never agreed to it. Josie had to leave, and it had all worked out for the best in the end.

Could Abigail learn to let go and trust that God would work things out like He always had?

"Please, Isaac," she said. "Let's work through this together. I want to be there for you."

"But I yelled at you," Isaac said. "I lost my temper, and I didn't think through what I was saying before I said it."

Abigail patted the seat next to her. "Sit."

Though he hesitated, he did as she asked.

"Yes, you did yell at me. However, as long as I've known you, I've only seen you yell at someone twice. Once when you were frustrated with a little boy bullying a little girl then lashing out at me, and the second time when you were highly emotional, upset with me and trying to make me see reason."

Isaac nodded slowly. "So what you're saying is when I'm with you, I can't think straight or rationally. That doesn't bode well for my ability to love others."

The pain and fear in his voice was that of the little boy who'd bounced around so much from family to family and didn't know how to love or be loved.

Maybe, like everything else they had in common, they both had to learn how to open up. Could they learn it together?

"Or maybe it shows you that when you finally start letting yourself care for someone, you're able to access more of your emotions, and that's something you've never done before. So maybe, rather than doing what you've always done and stuffing them down, pretending you don't feel anything, see what we can do to work through them. Together."

She didn't even want to think about the elephant in the room, that at the end of the summer, he would be gone. But God had put them together in this situation for a reason, and she couldn't push him away when he needed her the most just because she was afraid of what the future would hold.

Wasn't that what was causing all of their problems? Their fears?

That realization brought an even greater sense of peace to Abigail. How many of her decisions were based on her fear of the future? She couldn't know what was going to happen or how it was all going to play out. So why did she let those worries control her? Why was she letting those worries keep her from loving someone like Isaac?

Abigail hadn't noticed Brady leave the room for a box of tissues, but she was grateful when he handed them to her.

"Communicating in relationships takes work," Brady said. "It's like anything else. It's a skill you learn."

Maddie nodded. "It sure is. I'm not proud of how I acted when Brady and I were first together, and the truth is, the only way I knew how to communicate with him was by yelling. It was all I knew from the house

I grew up in, and even though we thankfully never got married, we made a conscious decision to be partners in raising our daughter, and that included going to some parenting and communication classes."

A pained look crossed Maddie's face, and Abigail felt an even deeper sympathy for the woman they'd brought into their family. "And, of course, when the truth about everything I lied about came to light, it took even more counseling, which also included more work on communication. I know we don't always get it right, but it helps when we both know that we're on the same team, and the most important thing in our lives is what's best for Kayla."

Then Maddie looked at Abigail. "I'm certainly not one to give expert advice. But I do know that you both care for each other, so I encourage you to make it work. You've both gone to school to learn about dealing with people. I know that none of this communication stuff is news to either of you."

Turning her attention to Isaac, Maddie continued, "I don't know everything you've been through, but I do know I had a hard childhood, too. My mom was the town drunk, and I never knew my father. I made a lot of really bad choices as a result. But once I had Kayla, I made the decision to make better choices because I didn't want to pass that on to her."

Even though she wasn't sure she and Isaac were okay yet, Abigail reached over and grabbed Isaac's hand. "Do you see? All of us here are healing from bad experiences in our past. They aren't the same, but we know that healing alone doesn't bring true healing. I'm choosing to love you through this. Yes, you yelled at me, and yes, I cried. But you also forced me to face a truth I have been avoiding for years."

She gave a self-deprecating chuckle as she looked at her sister and cousin, then at Brady. "They will all tell you that they've gotten on me multiple times over the years about needing to let go of control and not feel like I have to do everything myself."

Then she squeezed Isaac's hand. "But until you came along, I didn't realize that I've actually been hurting myself. I give and I give and I give, but I don't take care of me."

Abigail took a deep breath. "So let's do this. I'm going to let go of my need to control what happens at the stables and the fear that something bad will happen if I'm not here to watch over things, and you're going to see your father, and we're both going to trust that God is in control."

Who were these people? Isaac couldn't believe the outpouring of support coming from Abigail's family. No one, aside from Mr. P, had ever stepped up like that for him. As Isaac looked around the room, he saw the compassion and caring on the faces of people he'd only met a few short weeks ago.

He looked at Maddie, who was taking vacation time from her job so he could be with his father. They had only had a few conversations, nothing deep and nothing to make them close, and yet here she was, sacrificing for him. But perhaps that was the result of the compassionate love she'd been shown.

All his life, he'd been told that you had to earn love, to do all the right things, and maybe then you'd be worthy of love. But even then, he'd always felt like he owed people something as a result.

He hadn't done anything spectacular for these people, and yet, they were doing all this for him.

Isaac looked at Abigail.

He'd been kind of a jerk in how he'd spoken to her, but all he saw was compassion in her eyes.

More importantly, he realized that this was what he'd been searching for his whole life. This was what family looked like. People coming together and working through their problems instead of just fighting and treating each other badly.

"I can't believe the support I'm getting from you all," Isaac said quietly. "I don't know how to properly say thank-you."

Abigail's smile made him wonder again if there was a way for things between them to work out. Maybe if she could go with him and see that it was okay to leave her family. Or at the very least, after seeing how the family all worked together to make this trip happen, they could work together to find a way to make a relationship work.

"There's no need to thank any of us. This is what family is for," she said.

They'd made him a part of the family. He hadn't asked; he hadn't tried. But they chose to include him anyway.

If Abigail could see him as family, was it possible that she could see him as something more?

Isaac shook his head. Definitely not the

appropriate time to think about such things. But perhaps, on their trip together, they could find a way to connect, and God would help them find a way to navigate these feelings that kept coming up.

Camp Guffey was his future. But more and more, he couldn't imagine a future without these amazing people.

Chapter Eleven

Isaac still couldn't believe he was sitting here in the hospital with his father. The tired old man bore no resemblance to the imposing figure who'd frequented Isaac's nightmares. The cancer had caused him to deteriorate so badly that it was like looking at a wrinkled old child.

As much as he'd always said he would hate the man forever, as he looked at the wasting body, he found that he didn't have the energy to do so. All he felt was pity for the pathetic creature lying in the bed.

"Thank you for coming," his father said. "I know I don't deserve it, and you've made it clear over the years how you felt about me, but I want you to know that I've always loved you."

Loved? Isaac felt his body tense at the word, and Abigail took his hand. She didn't have to speak for him to know that she was encouraging him to trust God in this moment.

His father gestured at a box on the bedside table. "I saved all the letters you sent back, so if you ever want to read them, they're yours. I don't have much in the way of a legacy or even an estate to give you, but I hope I can bring you some kind of peace, closure or whatever you need from me to live a happy life."

Isaac had never thought about needing anything from his father to live a happy life. All he'd thought he'd needed was to be far away from this man and to never have anything to do with him again. But having spent time in prayer, in study and talking with Abigail on the way here, he knew that as long as he held unforgiveness in his heart toward his father, he'd always be a prisoner of his hatred. He'd never thought he needed peace or closure, but as he thought about all the things he tried not to be, Isaac knew there was one thing he needed.

"How do I not make the mistakes you did?" He looked over to Abigail, feeling so much love for her, even though everything was so messed up between them, and he didn't know how they would ever find their way to be together.

Even though Abigail had forgiven him for yelling at her, Isaac still feared that, one day, he would lose control the way his father had and do something to seriously harm her. Maybe the person he was most trying to avoid being like was the person who could help him learn how to prevent that from happening.

"I loved you," his father said. "I loved your mother. But I wasn't good at dealing with my feelings. I wasn't good at swallowing my pride. I wasn't good at taking my troubles to the Lord and relying on Him. I thought everything was on me, and I never let God do the work."

The old man reached for Isaac like he wanted to take his hand, and even though Isaac had thought that he would never want to touch his father like that, he took it anyway. His father's hand felt tiny and weak in his own, and Isaac found himself releasing the hate he'd felt all these years.

"I thought it was enough to say a prayer to ask God to save me," his father continued. "But I didn't realize that following the Lord is about making the decision in every moment to honor Him. Being a man of God isn't about that one big decision, but about all the little decisions along the way."

Isaac gave his father's hand a gentle squeeze, trying not to hurt the man who'd hurt him so much over the years.

If you'd told Isaac even a month ago that he'd treat the man with such care, he'd have laughed in your face. He couldn't explain it, but he felt like God was right there with him, giving him the strength to do this.

The old man looked like every word was draining more of his life from him, but Isaac could see the determination in his face to get the words out. "If you want to avoid the mistakes I made, remember that every moment is a chance to make a choice. If you make the wrong choice one moment, you always have the next moment make the right one."

His father closed his eyes briefly, but then they fluttered open, and he spoke again. "My mistake was not knowing that, and thinking that because I made the wrong choice one moment, I was stuck with that choice. Each moment is an opportunity. Rather than beating yourself up for making the wrong choice in the last moment, use it as fuel to make the right choice in the next."

Isaac noticed that Abigail had tears in her eyes. He thought about how he had yelled at her, and how he'd allowed the guilt over that mistake to cause him to pull away from her. Instead, she'd worked through it with him.

He didn't have to be like his father. Maybe he would make those bad choices, but his father was right; his next choice could be a good one.

And wasn't that what he taught the kids he worked with? You always had the chance to make a better choice.

His father gripped his hand tightly as though he was clinging to a lifeline.

"I'm sorry," his father rasped. "I thought that yelling at you or hitting you as well as your mother was the way to get you to do what I wanted. It's how I was raised, and it's all I knew."

His father coughed, a movement that shook his whole body despite the weakness of the cough. "It's no excuse, but I didn't know any better. I wish I did. I wish to God I had."

Tears rolled down his face, and Isaac recognized this was a broken old man who bitterly regretted his choices in life.

There was no excuse for how his father had treated him, and it was clear that the guilt the old man lived with was far worse than any punishment Isaac could've imagined for him. For the first time, Isaac understood what Abigail had been trying to communicate to him when she'd told him to let go of all the things he'd held against his father.

The dying man in the hospital bed wasn't the monster Isaac remembered. He'd built him up as an evil person for so long that Isaac hadn't been able to see the truth. His father was just a lonely, lost man who handled his anger in hurtful ways. Isaac didn't have to be that. Sure, his father's blood ran through his veins, and that same abuse was what had shaped him as a person.

Unlike his father, Isaac had the chance to make a different choice. He remembered what Abigail had said to him about how he could have hurt Gabe, how he could have done all of these inappropriate things, but Isaac had made the choice not to. In fact, the choice to do harm to someone hadn't occurred to him except as something he didn't want to do.

Isaac had choices, and he no longer feared

being a monster because he understood what those choices were.

He didn't have to be like his father.

And as he stared at the old man, who lived with the regrets of his poor choices, Isaac realized that he didn't have to carry the burden of hating him anymore.

Even if his father hadn't expressed regret over his actions, Isaac could see how holding on to the pain his father had caused only hurt Isaac. He'd been trapped in fear, and now he could see freedom.

"I forgive you, Dad," Isaac said.

The old man's eyes teared up, and then they closed. Abigail put her arm around Isaac and rested her head on his shoulder.

"That was beautiful," she said. "Thank you for encouraging me to be a part of this."

They sat in silence for a few minutes, then the nurse came in to tell them their visiting time was up. As they left the room, Isaac felt the remainder of his burdens wash away. He thanked God, not only for giving him the strength to face his father, but also for helping him to see the truth.

Isaac did love Abigail. While he didn't know how they could be together, he knew that his choice would be to love her, and to work through whatever obstacles they faced. But could he get her to see that their love was something special and worth fighting for?

On the way back to Camp Guffey, where they were staying at Mr. P's house on the edge of camp, Isaac received a phone call from the prison infirmary. His father had passed away shortly after they left.

Though Isaac didn't feel the grief of losing someone he cared for deeply, he did feel a slight twinge of regret he hadn't been expecting. He'd always thought he'd be elated, knowing such an evil man no longer walked this earth. Instead, he felt sadness for a man who'd made so many bad choices in life. More importantly, Isaac felt a sense of peace, knowing that he had found closure and a release from the grudge he'd carried for so long.

Abigail held Isaac's hand as they drove to Camp Guffey. He'd been quiet since receiving the news of his father's passing, so Abigail was doing her best to support him with prayer and silent comfort. They'd remain here a couple more days to make arrangements for his father, and Abigail was going to use this time to focus on her relationship with Isaac and support him.

She glanced at her phone, resisting the temptation to check in and make sure everything was okay back at the stables. It wasn't that she didn't trust her family; they all knew what they were doing. Other than a few quick overnight trips to watch Wyatt compete in rodeos and help Laura, Abigail hadn't really been gone from the stables this long since the days when the various stable riding acts would travel to compete. But that was a long time ago, and that was work, so Abigail could honestly say that this was the first time she'd ever left home to do something for herself.

Camp Guffey was only a short distance from the infirmary where Isaac's father had been. Mr. P—or Fred, as he'd insisted Abigail call him—had invited them to stay with him in his home since the camp was underway and full of campers for the summer.

Abigail loved the bright, cheery home on the edge of Lake Guffey, for which Camp Guffey was named. As soon as they arrived, Abigail felt a sense of warmth, very much like how she felt at the stables. No wonder Isaac had so easily fit in there.

Once Abigail was settled into her charming room, Isaac walked her over to the camp. "I want to give you a tour of the place I love

so much," he said, his voice so full of pride
that once again Abigail wondered if it was
foolish for them to even consider having a
relationship when it was clear she couldn't
ask him to give this place up.

"I never thought I'd get to see Camp
Guffey," she said. "I can't wait to hear all
about it."

As he walked her through the camp, point-
ing out the various buildings and activities,
Abigail immediately began taking mental
notes on things they could do at Shepherd's
Creek. True, Camp Guffey was a sleepaway
camp, and they only held a day camp, but
she could see some of the activities trans-
lating well.

Though if Abigail was honest, she'd also
say that she was looking for places here
where they could have horses. These kids
could benefit from some horse lessons as
well. A silly thought, since Isaac had barely
overcome his fear of horses, but you never
knew how things could work out.

It was an idyllic place, and Abigail could
see why Isaac loved it so much. While they
barely had a green season at all in Colorado, everything here in Minnesota was a
lush shade of the color unlike anything Abi-

gail had ever seen. Absolutely gorgeous. The lake so peaceful and tranquil, Abigail felt herself drawn to it.

"Do you mind if we go down by the lake?"

Isaac took her by the hand. Even though they'd held hands several times today, that had been for emotional comfort. This felt deeper, more special. She wanted to say that they shouldn't do this, but who was she kidding, she was already in too deep, and Isaac had her heart. How she was supposed to handle this, she didn't know, because as much as they'd been willing to admit that they had feelings for each other, there was still the practicality of how to make something work between them.

They walked to a small cove, which led them to another path by the lake. Even though it was meant as a trail for the kids at the camp, Abigail could see how it would also make for a peaceful romantic walk. But as always when she thought of romance with Isaac, her heart was torn.

Once again, she felt the nudge of the spirit of God telling her to be patient and trust that things would work out. She supposed they had this trip, and the rest of the summer, to see what the future held.

As they walked, Isaac told her more about Camp Guffey, and even though Abigail had heard some of the stories before, it was different hearing them in the place he loved.

Being here with him, listening to the lap of the waves against the shoreline, Abigail could honestly say there was no place she'd rather be. Though part of her still faced the temptation of wanting to call home, the truth was she didn't miss it nearly as much as she'd thought she would.

After a while, Isaac held out his hand. "I want to show you something."

He led her down a path toward what looked like a giant garage.

"This is Mr. P's shop. Since I just have a small apartment in Colorado, and this is my true home, he lets me keep my larger stuff here, so I thought I'd show you the things that are special to me."

When they went into the shop, Abigail was surprised by all the stuff in it. It was like the shop they had at the stables, only with more equipment and the ability to do more things. The guys would have a field day in there. Maybe someday, they could work it out so everyone could come here and experience this place.

Though she initially dismissed it as a silly thought, she also wondered if maybe during the off-season, they could figure something out. The truth was they'd never thought about it, so how would they know if they didn't try?

It was amazing how quickly her mind had opened up to the possibilities. Even though his father's words had been for Isaac, Abigail had been thinking a lot about the idea of choices, and how, where she'd always felt like she had no other choice, maybe there were ones that existed that she'd never considered.

Isaac led her over to a corner, and when he pulled off the tarp, she spied a collection of motorcycles.

"These are amazing," she said.

Isaac beamed with pride. "They're my babies."

He pointed to the one closest to them. "This was the first motorcycle I ever bought with my own money," he said. "It was a piece of junk, but I spent hours working on it, finding parts in the junkyards, rebuilding everything. No one thought I could get a piece of junk running, but I did it."

He ran his hand over the bike like it was a treasured possession.

"Does it still run?" Abigail asked.

Isaac nodded. "You'd better believe it. I take this baby out every time I'm here. Gotta keep the engine running smooth."

He looked at her, a gleam in his eye. "You want to go for a spin?"

"I've never been on a motorcycle before."

"So let's give it a try," Isaac said.

Abigail hesitated.

"That's right," Isaac said. "You've always been afraid."

At least he understood.

"You know there's only one way to face your fear, right?" Isaac asked.

She should have known he was going to go there. And even though getting on that motorcycle was the last thing Abigail wanted to do, she also knew that after his bravery in riding Simba and facing his father, the least she could do was follow his example.

"Okay," she said.

He got them helmets, and then he took her on a ride around the lake.

It was one of the most beautiful views she'd had, almost like being on horseback, except a little lower to the ground and faster. But still, it was a different level of detail than you saw riding in a car or taking a walk.

At the beginning of the ride, Abigail was practically shaking. But as the ride continued, she felt safer and more confident as she wrapped her arms around Isaac.

She also finally understood what he'd meant about how the motorcycle, while also being dangerous, gave him more control than a horse. Everything was on him to not make a mistake, even though that sense of control was also an illusion, since another driver could cause an accident. Abigail had thought that she was safe in riding a horse because even though the horse had a mind of its own, she'd built a relationship with the animal that kept her safe.

But that safety, too, was an illusion.

Even in this short time away, she was seeing how they all clung to ideas of safety and control and what they thought would give them that. But none of it, aside from their relationship with God, was real.

Could she let her family do more at the stables so she could travel like this? Could she and Isaac find a way to make their relationship work?

She didn't know, but maybe it was time to try.

They stopped at a spot near the lake, and

it reminded Abigail a lot of her own favorite spot at the stables.

"This is amazing," Abigail said.

Isaac grinned. "Now you know why I like your rock so much," he said.

Abigail smiled at him and let him put his arms around her. "This is really a beautiful place," she said.

He looked at her so tenderly that she knew he wanted to kiss her. All of her reasons for them not being together still existed, and yet, she felt like she owed it to them both to see what would happen. Abigail loved Isaac, and together they'd found the strength to face their fears and overcome them.

Surely God wouldn't have brought them this far if He didn't have in mind some way for them to be together. She had to have faith that if only they trusted in their love and in God, they would find a way.

So when Isaac kissed her, she allowed herself to be enveloped in his embrace, and prayed for God's strength to help them make their relationship work.

Chapter Twelve

Though Abigail had hoped to be back in time for some of the classes that week, travel delays had them pulling up at the stables just as parents were arriving for pickup Friday afternoon.

Several adults were gathered in a semi-circle, talking to Josie and Brady angrily. As Abigail mentally checked off who all the adults were, a sinking feeling hit her stomach. Gabe's parents. Katie's dad and stepmom. Josh's parents.

Isaac reached for her hand and gave it a squeeze. "It's going to be okay."

The familiar feeling of panic that hit every time Abigail gave up control of something only to have it explode in her face filled her chest. They had known the kids were having issues, so why had Abigail thought it was going to be okay to leave?

She pulled her hand away from his and opened the door. "Don't tell me what it is or isn't going to be. I let you talk me into leaving, just for a few days. Look at this. Everything is a mess."

When she reached the group, she saw Gabe sitting on the picnic bench, an ice pack to his face. Katie and Josh were sitting next to one another, looking triumphant.

Josh's dad had his hand on his son's shoulder, looking proud.

Gabe's father immediately pounced on Abigail. "What kind of place are you running here? These children terrorized my son. His nose was bleeding, and he's going to have a black eye."

Abigail looked over at Katie and Josh, then back at him. "What happened?"

"I'll tell you what happened," Gabe's father said. "It's what I just told you. These two children terrorized my poor son."

"That's not what happened," Josie said coldly. She turned to Abigail. "Gabe was picking on Josh as usual. Katie told him to stop, and Gabe told her to make him, so Katie pushed Gabe into a pile of manure."

Josie turned to Katie. "We know that was the wrong thing to do, don't we?"

Katie shrugged. "He had it coming. He's been picking on poor Josh from day one. Today was the last straw. He took Josh's pocket dinosaur and threw it into the pile of manure. And he called Josh a bad name."

This wouldn't have happened if Abigail had been there. She'd seen the way Gabe had been picking on Josh, and she did everything she could to separate the boys and to defuse the situation when Gabe was being particularly mean. It wasn't that she had anything against Josie and Maddie, but they didn't know the children the way she did.

Josh stood up. "Gabe got so mad that Katie pushed him in the manure that he hit her." The quiet little boy who only wanted to be left alone to play with his dinosaurs clenched his fists tightly at his sides. "Everyone knows you don't hit girls."

Josh's dad ruffled his hair and said, "That's my boy."

It figured that it would take an incident like this for Josh's family to finally be proud of him, yet it still shouldn't have happened.

Abigail looked at him. "So what did you do?"

Josh squared his shoulders. "What any man would do. I protected my friend."

Josh took a step toward Gabe. "And for the record, you fight like a girl. You can say mean things to people, you can hit girls, but when someone your size comes for you, you can't take it."

Oh boy. All this time, they'd been encouraging Josh to find courage, but this was not the way to go about it. Abigail glanced at Isaac to gauge his reaction, but she couldn't read his expression. Why had she followed her heart?

"Hey," Katie said. "Girls can fight good, too. I gave him that black eye."

Josh immediately relaxed. "Yeah, you're right. Besides, Isaac has been saying that it's not okay to say mean things about girls, and saying that he fights like a girl is mean. I'm sorry. Between the both of us, I think Gabe learned his lesson."

Abigail shook her head. "By fighting? That's not how we resolve our differences here, children."

"Exactly," Gabe's father said. "I'm going to be filing a complaint against your facility with the state for allowing such violence against my son."

A complaint? With the state? Abigail's stomach sank. She took just a few days for herself, and now everything she'd worked for was in jeopardy. She wanted to cry, but tears wouldn't help the situation.

"Mr. Booth, I am sure we can work this out without getting the authorities involved. It is unfortunate that your son was in a fight. We've sent letters home about the disagreements with the children, so maybe now it's time we figure out a way we can work this all out together."

Gabe's father pulled a card out of his pocket. "Oh, I don't think so," he said. "I trusted you to take care of my son, and instead, he faces wild abuse from these two hooligans."

When Abigail looked at the business card, her stomach sank even further. She'd known Gabe's father was fairly well-off. What she didn't realize was he was a partner in one of those law firms on television commercials that promised to get you the most money for your lawsuit.

She didn't notice Isaac had come to stand behind her.

"Marshall," he said. "Nice to see you again."

Gabe's father stared at him for a second. "Do I know you?"

Isaac squared his shoulders. "You don't remember me, do you?"

Gabe's father shook his head. "Why would I? Were you someone my firm sued who lost?"

Abigail closed her eyes and prayed for God's protection and provision. Knowing what she knew about Isaac's past, this could be anything, and because Isaac wasn't familiar with how they did things here and had only just become a Christian, she had no idea what was going to come next. *Please, God make this okay.*

"Isaac Johnston." He held out his hand to the other man. "I was a little foster kid who stayed at your home years ago. We were about the same age as these kids. I remember how you used to beat me up."

A stunned silence washed over all the adults.

Marshall gave Isaac a long look, then said, "Oh yeah. I remember you now. Scrawny little brat with his nose in a book all the time. Looks like you finally filled out and grew up. Good for you. What does that have to do with anything here? Those children assaulted my son, and I'm going to see justice."

"Where was the justice for me when you assaulted me?" Isaac said quietly.

Marshall laughed. "We were just kids. You are way too sensitive."

Isaac shook his head. "And they are just kids. What's this really about? Until today, I didn't know Gabe was your son. But now, it makes perfect sense. He has the same MO you did when we were kids."

Abigail's heart sank. For all their work on forgiveness, Isaac was once again having to face a painful part of his past. Worse, whatever happened here could impact Abigail's future. If it hadn't already.

This was why she never should have left. All this talk of getting out there and doing things for herself, it was all nonsense.

Isaac turned his attention to Gabe, who had stopped crying and was silently watching. No longer did he have the ice pack pressed to his face, like he was trying to get sympathy, but he was studying the interaction between the adults.

Even though he didn't like the things the boy had done, Isaac felt sympathy for him. Given Marshall's attitude and the way the boy cowered, it wasn't hard to guess that

Gabe's misbehavior was his way of finding power in a world where he felt otherwise powerless.

Isaac looked over at Marshall in his expensive suit that didn't fit in here. As kids, he used to brag about how big and powerful and important he'd be. Funny how the child had never really grown up.

"You're just mad because your son finally got his comeuppance," Isaac said. "That's always how it has been with you. Anything to win. When we were kids, if I succeeded in getting you in trouble for what you did to me, you always found a way to get me back harder, so much so that it was never worth it for me to try to get justice for myself."

Abigail started to speak, but Isaac shook his head. He knew she was probably quaking in her boots, terrified that Marshall was going to destroy the place she loved, but Isaac knew better. Marshall only preyed on those he perceived as being weaker than him. Isaac was no longer that weak child, and he wasn't going to let this man ruin everything Abigail had worked so hard for.

Isaac continued, "You were really good at hiding my bruises so that people couldn't see what you'd done to me, or you'd make sure that there'd be some other rational explanation for how I'd gotten hurt. Is that what you do to your son? Most kids who are bullies have parents who bully them."

The good news, as Isaac had learned, was that people who were bullies always had a choice. Isaac could have followed the examples given to him, but instead, he'd chosen a different path.

"That's slander," Marshall said.

Isaac shrugged "I haven't been to law school, but I know it doesn't meet the definition of slander. I'm just asking questions here. Wondering what Gabe would say if we asked him about things at home."

"You have no right to talk to my son about our home," Marshall said.

Once again, Isaac shrugged, trying to ignore the way Gabe's mom seemed nervous. "No, I can't investigate your family. But if I hear so much as one word about you filing charges against these kids or their families, or against the stables, or even a hint that an investigation into them has been opened, I'll make sure that the people who do have the right to ask him some questions pay you a visit."

Even if Marshall didn't file any complaints, Isaac would be watching. So far, other than this series of arguments, Isaac had no reason to believe Gabe was being abused, but now that he had this information, he'd be watching the boy more closely.

Gabe's mother started to cry.

"Please, Marshall. I think we all need to go home and calm down."

"Don't tell me what to do," Marshall said.

Josie had moved over to stand next to Gabe's mother. "You do need to calm down, and if you are threatening her or Gabe, I will have no problem calling the authorities and finding a safe place for them to go."

She put her arm around Gabe's mother. "Do you feel threatened by your husband? Or feel that he's a threat to your son?"

The woman swallowed—an exaggerated movement that they all saw—looked at her husband, then at Josie, then at the ground. "Everything's fine," she said. "I think we all just need to take some space."

"You see?" Marshall looked like his blood was about to boil. "She said everything's fine. Your unfounded accusations aren't going to save you from the authorities when I call them about this place."

Brady stepped forward. "Do it. Call the

authorities. I have nothing to hide. Everything is well-documented, as it should be."

Having been through the training and done his own documentation on the fights between the children, Isaac had the same faith that Brady did. But when he glanced at Abigail, he saw the fear in her eyes.

She'd been so angry with him when she came home and realized there was a problem. He knew she was blaming herself, but how could he get her to see that none of this was her fault?

Now, with this crisis before them, could Isaac convince Abigail that their love was worth the risk?

Gabe's mom nudged her husband, like she, at least, understood that Marshall's threats weren't going to get them anywhere. "Please, let's just go home."

For the first time, Marshall looked defeated. "So what you're saying here is this was just a misunderstanding between kids," he said.

All of the adults murmured in agreement. Though Isaac would have preferred to press the point about Gabe's behavior, the poor child likely suffered enough. This was more than a simple misunderstanding, but if it calmed the situation for now, they could revisit it later with cooler heads.

Marshall gestured to his son. "Get your things. We're going home."

The little boy grabbed his backpack, shooting furtive glances at Katie and Josh, and Isaac thought he saw him mouth the words *I'm sorry* before he joined his parents and slowly trudged toward their car. Maybe Gabe had learned something after all.

As the family pulled out of the parking lot, no one said a word, but then Josh's dad spoke. "I feel bad for that boy," he said turning to Isaac, sympathy on his face. "You got bullied by his dad as a kid?"

Isaac nodded. "I did. It's why I'm very sensitive to children who get bullied. I know what it was like, getting picked on and having no one stand up for me."

Then Isaac turned his attention to the kids. "I'm glad you finally stood up to Gabe, but what you did was wrong. We can't use violence to solve our problems. No matter what happens, we always have a choice, so we need to make good ones."

Katie and Josh nodded slowly.

"I could have gone and punched Marshall in the nose after all these years. But instead,

I chose to talk to him, and I tried to do the right thing."

He looked at Abigail, who looked like she was ready to cry. He prayed that God would give her comfort and help her see that everything was going to be okay. None of this was her fault for leaving.

But he also wanted to make sure the kids felt okay as well.

"I'm sorry Gabe threw your dinosaur in the manure pile," Isaac said, pulling a tiny dinosaur out of his own pocket. "I still have the one you gave me when I rode Simba, so if you want it back, you can have it."

Josh shook his head. "No. You, Katie and Abigail are the only ones who understand my love for dinosaurs. I want you to have it. I've got more at home."

Josh's father looked at his son. "I thought if I could make you a horseman, then the kids wouldn't pick on you, because I see the way they do. I kept thinking I just needed to toughen you up, but you just needed someone who accepted that you like dinosaurs."

This, too, was a benefit of today's mess. Isaac looked over at Abigail to see if she realized it as well, but her face was full of so many emotions, he couldn't tell if she understood.

Josh stood a little taller than she'd ever seen him when discussing the dinosaur thing with his father.

"Yes, sir." Josh gestured at Katie. "But Katie says that sometimes to find dinosaur bones you have to ride horses, so I'm trying to give them a chance."

Josh's father turned to Katie. "Thank you, young lady." Then he smiled up at her parents. "Josh was telling me about his friend Katie who might not get to go to the next session of camp because of her dad's job and her stepmom being unable to take her, so I'd like to talk to you folks about carpooling or something so Katie can come. She's been a good friend to my son, and I don't want him to lose that because you can't work out transportation issues."

Katie's stepmother started to cry. "Thank you," she said. "I know Katie thinks I'm just being mean, but I have so many responsibilities. It's easier if the neighbor watches her, even though Katie says it's boring. But if you could help us by giving her rides, that would be a weight off of my back."

Katie was obviously too young to understand the way sometimes people broke under the pressure of too many responsibilities, but Isaac wondered if maybe her stepmother was like Abigail, taking on too much and not taking time for herself.

Katie looked over at her family. "I could go to camp again? You mean it?"

Her dad looked over at Josh's dad, then down at her. "We've got some details to work out, but yes, sweetheart, if these fine folks are willing to help us get you here, I think we can make it work."

Katie looked at all the adults around her, then she hugged her dad, saying, "Thank you. Thank you."

Her dad hugged her back and kissed the top of her head. "There's someone else you should thank, too."

Katie released her father and walked over to her stepmother. "You're really letting me go to camp?"

Her stepmother bent down to Katie's level. "It was never about me not wanting you to go. But with my job and taking care of my sick mother and the stuff I do for the neighbor down the street, I don't have enough time to bring you here every day. I want you to be around the horses, I just didn't know how to make it work."

Isaac observed Abigail's family standing here in support of the situation and wondered if she realized that the support she gave all of them was available to her. Even though she'd thought it had all been a disaster, Isaac saw how they'd all worked together. Could he get Abigail to see that and not shut down what they'd begun?

Chapter Thirteen

After things died down, information was exchanged and everyone got on their way, Abigail let the tears flow.

Even though she'd loved her time in Minnesota, her place was here, taking care of the people who needed her. It was foolish to think that she could leave and follow a bunch of silly dreams. This was why she could only wish about traveling to a beach and putting her feet in the sand. She'd only been gone a few days, and everything had fallen apart.

Isaac came over and tried to hug her, but she pushed him away.

"Please, don't. None of this would've happened if you hadn't talked me into going to Minnesota with you."

"That's nonsense," Josie said. "Every single one of us knew that a fight between Gabe and Josh was inevitable. It just so happened to occur on our watch. It could easily have happened with you here, and it would've been the same result."

Abigail shook her head. "Marshall could put the stables under investigation, and we could lose everything we've worked for."

Maddie shook her head and held up her clipboard. "I have everything documented from today, plus I know Isaac left good notes. Let them come. We can prove our innocence. Besides, I think he's just full of hot air."

Though Maddie worked at a care facility, she didn't know what was at stake because none of it was on her. "Maybe he's making idle threats, but do you know how much time and resources an investigation takes? We finally have the resources to develop the program we've been dreaming of. This is going to set us back so far."

"So what?" Brady asked. "We don't need a big program to be successful at what we do. Sure, we've grown and are seeing success unlike ever before. But maybe this is a sign we need to think about what we're really trying to accomplish here. You shouldn't feel guilty for leaving for a few days."

Brady looked at her with such tenderness. Of all the people here, he'd worked with her the longest, been through the most as they'd seen the ups and downs of the stables. She couldn't believe Brady, of all people, was saying that their growth was bad. She stared at him.

"Don't look at me like that," Brady said. "You did what you set out to do. You got us all back together, and the stables aren't in danger of going under anymore. Sure, if we have to face the time and expense of a drawn-out investigation because some fancy-pants lawyer has it out for us, it'll hurt. So what? We have each other, and even if we stop doing the camps entirely, and just focus on what we've always done, we'll be fine."

Abigail stared at him. "But it was your dream to grow the stables. And Josie's. And now that Laura and Wyatt are here, we can do all the things."

Josie put her arm around Abigail. "All the things my father wanted to do. Or actually, even more."

What was Josie saying here? "But we had to do this so that your job would let you stay here, and we need to be able to support all the family so they can be here, too," Abigail said.

Didn't they see? This wasn't about fulfilling Uncle Joe's dreams for the stables, but about keeping the family together.

"Honestly, now that I'm home and I have a husband and a family, I'm starting to rethink my priorities," Josie said. "We haven't shared this with anyone yet, but I've been running the numbers, and I'm seriously considering quitting my job with the rec center in Denver because my heart isn't there anymore. I love the children, and I love working with the programs, but I don't love the time I'm spending away from my family."

Though Abigail knew Josie was saying that to make her feel better, it only felt like more pressure to Abigail. Now the stables had to have more income to provide for Josie to have a job.

"But then we need—"

"Stop," Josie said. "I see that little hamster wheel turning in your head. The stables don't need to provide any extra to make this happen. Brady's current salary is enough to support us all. As a test, I have put everything I've made from my job into savings since I found out I was pregnant, because I knew I wanted to spend as much time as I could with my baby. We haven't spent any of my salary in all this time. We don't need the stables to give me a job. You don't need to worry about how you're going to find enough money to make it all work."

Then her expression softened as she took Abigail's hands. "Besides that, it isn't your responsibility to make sure that our family has income. I'm a grown-up now, and you don't have to provide for me. It's okay for you to let go and let all of us out into the world, fending for ourselves. You did your job. If making the stables into this big amazing program and continuing to grow it is what you want, then of course I'm on board with you. But is that what you want? Have you thought about what you really want from life?"

In all her years, no one had ever asked Abigail that question. She thought about her vision board in her office with all the travel pictures that Isaac kept pushing her on. She thought about the invitation to the wedding in Costa Rica that she hadn't been able to attend.

The truth was, all Abigail had ever known was the stables and the drive to make the stables the best it could be because that was what everyone expected of her. But what if that wasn't where she was supposed to be?

"I don't know what to do with that question," she said.

Even though she'd just pushed Isaac away, he came to her again, taking her hand. "It's what I've been telling you all along. You're so busy taking care of everyone else and seeing to their needs, I don't think you even know what yours are anymore. I caught a glimpse of your desires when we were in Minnesota. We rode around the lake, and you told me all the things you wanted to try and see and do. Your family's got this. They're going to be okay. Take the time for you."

Tears rolled down her face. "This is all I've known. I don't know how to start over. I'm not young anymore. Those dreams, those are for young people."

"Who says?" he asked. "Mr. P is eighty years old, and the first thing he's going to do when he retires is go see the Eiffel Tower. As long as you got life left in you, there's nothing you can't do."

Laura had arrived, holding Josie's crying baby. "I'm sorry to interrupt, but we're out of bottles, and someone is very hungry."

Josie took baby Shana, holding her close and soothing her. "Thank you."

She went and settled herself on the bench to feed Shana, and Abigail felt the weight of Isaac's stare on her as she watched Josie settle her child.

"Is that what this is about? Do you want a baby?" Isaac asked.

Abigail stared at him. "What makes you think that?"

He shrugged. "You have this look of longing on your face."

To be honest, Abigail had never even thought of that question because she always assumed it was so beyond her. "It doesn't matter. I'm too old."

Isaac laughed. "Plenty of women have babies in their forties. Sure, you might need a little more help from a doctor, but if you want a baby, then say you want a baby, and we'll do what it takes to make it happen."

Abigail stared at him. "You said you didn't want children of your own," she said.

She hadn't meant for those words to come out, but when she did, it made her realize that the only person she would ever consider having a baby with was Isaac. He was the only man she wanted to share her life with, regardless of her age. The thought of that terrified her.

Yes, she had been looking at Josie with longing. But not because of the baby. Because Josie knew what she wanted from life and had a supportive husband who'd helped her make it happen.

Abigail had never considered any of these things for herself, and until meeting Isaac, it hadn't occurred to her that not only did she want them, but she could have them.

Isaac couldn't believe that he had just encouraged someone to have a child, but as he realized how much Abigail had begun to mean to him, he knew he'd do anything for her.

"I always thought that was true. I thought I would never want a biological child. But what I do know is I would do anything to make your dreams come true, and that includes giving you a baby. I've learned this summer that I am not my father."

The smile she gave him told him that all was not lost. He'd made real progress, and it was because of her love that he felt so strong.

"When I lashed out in anger the other day," he continued, "I thought it meant I was like him, but you showed me that I also know how to choose differently. Something my father confirmed."

Obviously being around Abigail had made him more comfortable showing his emotions because he didn't feel bad about the tears he was shedding.

"I saw what happened with Marshall and Gabe, and as soon as we're done here, I will be making a call to ensure that little boy is safe. That could have been the proof that men turn into their fathers, but to me it's proof that we get to choose differently."

He gestured at Abigail, Josie and Laura, and even at Wyatt. "All of you grew up in a bad situation, but you managed to become good people, raising good families. None of you have ever harmed your children. If you can learn to live a different life, then so can I."

Isaac turned his attention back to Abigail. "I know you had all kinds of excuses for why you don't want to share your life with me. But none of them have to do with you not loving me. Say you don't love me, and I will never ask you again. If you love me, then I commit to you I will do everything I can to help make your dreams come true."

He took her hands in his. "I've never seen

you as being too old for me. I've never seen you as not being beautiful. All I see is this amazing, incredible woman who deserves to have her dreams come true, and I want nothing more than to be the man who does that for you."

The tears in Abigail's eyes gave him hope. "You'd really have a baby with me?"

Isaac nodded as he shifted his weight. "I don't know any other woman I would say that to, but yes. I would do anything for you."

He swallowed, said a quick prayer, then continued. "You've been right about so many things, including how God can redeem all of the bad things that happen in our lives if we let Him. You opened my heart to letting Him."

Josie finished feeding her baby and handed her to Brady, then walked over to Abigail.

"Listen to him. Isaac loves you. Don't throw away love because of some stupid pride and ideas of how you think things are supposed to be. I've told you before, and I'm going to tell you again now. What you two have is rare, and he is willing to risk facing every single one of his fears for you."

The baby started crying again, and Brady got a disgusted look on his face.

Josie laughed. "Guess it's time for a diaper change."

Abigail smiled and turned back to Isaac. "Truthfully, I don't really want a baby. I mean I love my nieces and nephews, but I like being able to give them back, especially when they need a diaper change. I can't travel the world with a baby. It's just one of those things that I look at when I see what I could have done with my life and wonder what has passed me by."

Though he knew this was a particular pain point for her, he also knew she was looking at it through the wrong lens.

"Come on. Mr. P is twice your age, and he's not too old to live his dreams. The man is eighty, and you two spent hours discussing his travel plans. Are you so decrepit in your forties that you're gonna let some eighty-year-old beat you at living your dreams?"

The ridiculousness of Abigail's excuses finally hit Isaac.

"All of this is just an excuse. You've lived in your safe little haven for so long that the truth is, you're the one who's afraid. We've spent all this time working through my fears, working through the kids' fears, some of your small fears, but the fear you won't face is your own. Living your dreams is a scary thing, but just like you were always by my side as I faced my fears, I'll be right here by yours."

This time, Isaac felt the change in Abigail as she looked around at her family. "You're right. I am afraid. I know I'm good at doing stuff here at the stables. But all those other things I want to do, I don't know if I'm good enough. What if I go to all those places, and I hate them? What if I leave my family and everything falls apart?"

He stepped forward and took her hands again. "Then we'll figure it out together. I know most of your life you had to do this all on your own."

Isaac let go of one of her hands and gestured at the people surrounding them. "But it's different now. Just like you've been there for all of them, they're here for you. I am here for you."

As Abigail's eyes filled with tears, Isaac put his arms around her. "You're not alone anymore," he said.

One by one, the rest of Abigail's family came and put their arms around them until they were in a giant group hug. Isaac felt all of the love and realized that as much as he thought they were all doing this for Abigail, this was also about him and receiving the love he had been seeking his entire life.

Abigail kind of squirmed out of his grasp, and the group hug broke away.

"Isaac, I do love you. It's foolish of me to say otherwise. Maybe I'm scared, but I also can't leave behind everything I've worked so hard to rebuild."

"You can, and you will," Josie said. "Look, I stayed initially to help save the stables because otherwise you were going to lose everything you've ever known. You would lose your home. And now, I need you to know that I'm also willing to sell the stables to send you on your way to your new home."

Abigail's sharp intake of breath made Isaac's stomach sink. Was this going to break up the family? Was everything he'd thought was finally solved so perfectly going to blow up?

"What are you saying?" Abigail asked.

Josie shrugged. "I only wanted to save the stables because I didn't think you had anything else. Sure, the stables are what brought us all back together and helped us heal as a family. But we don't need the stables anymore. Brady and I got back together, and we're happily married and have a family. Sure, this is his job, but he gets job offers all the time. Wyatt has enough money from his rodeo winnings that he only took the job at the stables as a way to stay close to Laura and the boys. But they're happy now, and their family is growing, and he doesn't need the income from the stables. You did this for us, and we don't need it anymore. So, if what it takes to get you to spread your wings and fly is for me to sell the stables, then I'll do just that."

Although the last thing Isaac wanted was to see Abigail hurt, he understood exactly why Josie was doing this. She was pushing Abigail out of her comfort zone but also letting her know that she'd accomplished everything she'd worked for, in terms of helping her family, and it was her turn to help herself. He just wished it didn't come with the look of devastation on Abigail's face.

Josie, too, seemed to understand that. "But if running the stables is your dream, then of course I'm not going to sell it. I don't actually want to sell it, because this place truly has brought the family back together. I hope that we always have the stables in some form to help all the future generations learn about horses, but also learn about love. That's what you've turned Shepherd's Creek into. It's not a place where we just develop skills with horses, but where we learn who we really are and what we really value. So the question is, who are you? What do you value?"

Abigail hesitated, then wiped her sleeve across her face and turned to Isaac. "I don't know the answers to those questions. Sure, I know my values, but I don't know what I want. Josie is right. My dream for the stables wasn't about the stables. It was about my family. I achieved that. So what's next?"

Isaac shrugged. "I don't know. Only you can answer that for you, but like I said before, I stand with you for whatever is next."

He'd already been willing to give everything else up, including his fear of becoming a father and passing on his genes.

But that left one thing he was clinging to. One more thing he could let go of to show Abigail just how much he loved her.

He took her hands again. "Like you, I have gone through school with one singular purpose of mind. Taking over Camp Guffey has been the only thing I have chased. But if that's not what you want, then I'm willing to discover a new dream, too. I got into this so I could help kids like me, and the other thing I learned this summer is I don't have to do that at Camp Guffey."

As he spoke, he felt God showing him the truth behind his words and his prayers.

"I didn't need Camp Guffey to help Josh. I helped Josh just by being me. As much as we might think that helping others looks like a specific vehicle or specific place, the truth is, if we're really living out our purpose, we can help others anywhere."

He looked into Abigail's eyes. "All I ever wanted is Camp Guffey. I thought that since that's what helped me, it was how I would help others. I can help others anywhere, doing anything. So if you don't want to move to Minnesota, we don't have to. I will go anywhere in the world, as long as it's with you."

Once again, Abigail started crying, and Isaac was starting to think he was actually pretty bad at this whole romance thing.

"You would give up Camp Guffey for me?"

Isaac nodded. "It isn't about the camp. It's about who I am. Mr. P had been trying to tell me that about my life all along, but it took you to show me that. I have no doubt in my mind that, regardless of where I am or what I'm doing, I am living out God's purpose for my life. But the thing that remains unchanged is I do not want to do it without you by my side."

As Abigail took in all the words, trying to process everything that was happening, she felt a strange sense of panic rising up inside her like she was losing control of everything. Had she done all this work for nothing?

Josie wanted to sell the stables again, and Isaac was talking about not doing Camp Guffey anymore, and it all seemed so overwhelming. But then she took a deep breath. Closed her eyes. And asked God to make sense of the whole of this because she was clearly doing a terrible job on her own.

Which is when what they'd actually been saying hit her.

Josie wanted Abigail's happiness and was willing to give up the stables to make it happen. Isaac also wanted her happiness, and not only was he willing to give up his vow to never father a child, but he'd give up the camp for her as well.

It was like the revelation she'd had about riding the motorcycle and the horses. Control and safety were just illusions, and the only thing you could do was trust in God and follow Him wherever He took you, even if you were afraid.

Just as she thought she was coming to grips with all of it, Isaac said, "Abigail, you have sacrificed yourself, all of your needs and desires, for so many years. I think back to everything everyone has said about what you've done to keep your family together. Now everyone is telling you the same thing. This is your turn. This is your time."

Abigail swallowed, still trying to comprehend what was happening. Everything she knew about living a godly life was about serving others. What did it mean to have a dream of her own?

"Don't you understand?" she asked. "I've never given consideration to what I wanted. I'm living the plan for my life. And now that everyone is telling me that I don't have to, I don't know what I want to do."

Isaac gave her a supportive smile. "That's okay. But you also have to understand that no matter what you want to do, you have all of us supporting you."

She'd never felt so loved as she did in this moment. She felt her family's gaze on her like she was the most important thing, even though that was never what she'd set out to be. And Isaac was the only person who had ever seen her beyond all the things she did for others and sought to be support for her.

"I don't want you to give up Camp Guffey for me," she said.

Then she looked around at the family. "You really would be okay if I left?"

Laura nodded. "Don't you see? Both me and Josie got to leave. We got to experience life outside the stables, and it helped us see that this is our true home. I know not everyone needs to leave to find that feeling, but give it a chance. Maybe you go to Camp Guffey and miss home so much that you decide to come back. It sounds like Isaac would be okay with that. But maybe you stay, and you find that you are living out a greater dream than you could have ever thought possible."

The warmth of her sister's gaze melted Abigail's heart. She'd spent her whole life protecting Laura, looking out for Laura, even being a surrogate parent to Laura once their mother died. She'd never thought that Laura would be the one to mother her.

Abigail turned back to Isaac. "Is that true? If I went with you, and I found that I missed home, we could come back?"

Isaac pulled her into his arms and hugged her tight. "I know this has been your home your whole life. I've spent my whole life looking for a home, being bounced from place to place, wondering if this would finally be the one. For me, I've learned that home isn't a place, but a person. My home is with you."

She looked up at him, and he kissed her tenderly.

Unlike the other times they'd kissed, Abigail didn't feel scared or apprehensive or wonder what she was doing, kissing him. Because this felt like the most right thing she'd ever done.

Isaac's words about home not being a place but a person filled her heart. As he broke the kiss and looked deep in her eyes, she knew it was true for her as well.

All the things that she'd hoped to do, the places she wanted to go, and even the person she now wanted to be, none of those mattered without him.

"All right," she said. "You've convinced me. It's time for me to leave Shepherd's Creek. It's time for me to discover what else in the world is out there for me."

She turned to her family. "I don't know

what it's like to take care of myself or be taken care of. But this seems to be the direction that God is leading me in, so okay. It's time to go."

She looked back at Isaac. "But don't you think we should get married first?"

Isaac laughed and pulled her close to him again. "I thought I was the one who was supposed to propose."

She kissed him softly, then said, "I don't care much which of us does the asking, as long as we both do the marrying."

Epilogue

The waves nipped at her toes, and Abigail couldn't stop smiling. Her first time at the ocean, and she was here with her husband, and she couldn't have imagined doing it without him.

She'd once looked at pictures of people on the beach, wishing it could be her, but not daring to believe she'd ever get the opportunity.

And here she was, living her dream.

"I know it's just Texas, nothing as exotic as Costa Rica. But once we get more settled at Camp Guffey, we can start planning and saving to cross off all the other places on your list," Isaac said. "However, I have a surprise for you."

Part of Abigail wanted to tell him that she

didn't need Costa Rica, or any of the other places on her list, because she'd already been so richly blessed.

But her time with Isaac had taught her that by not asking and not trying, she would never get anything she wanted. But if she shared the desires of her heart, the answer might be no, but it also might be yes. And even if it seemed as impossible as leaving Shepherd's Creek, with the love and help of her family, her husband and God, they could work together to make all her dreams come true—and more.

Even better, she could make the dreams of countless children, who simply needed to know they were loved, become realities beyond anything anyone ever expected.

"I don't need a surprise," Abigail said, smiling at him as he drew her closer. "But I'll gladly accept whatever you have to offer."

He kissed her gently, sending warmth through her that made her feel cherished and deeply loved. Isaac saw and loved her for all that she was, and every touch reminded her of that.

"I just got a call from that rancher friend of Wyatt's. On the way home, we're going to stop by and look at some horses he's got for sale."

"Horses?" Abigail pulled away and looked back at him. "What are we going to do with horses?"

He shrugged. "There's a spot near the workshop where I thought we could build a stable. It wouldn't be anything fancy like Shepherd's Creek, but I looked up the state requirements for having horseback riding at Camp Guffey, and I think we could make it work."

Abigail never would have imagined that the man who had been too terrified to ride a horse would now be looking at bringing horseback riding to Camp Guffey.

Isaac had left Shepherd's Creek at the end of the summer—degree in hand—to accept the position at Camp Guffey and make the transition from Mr. P to him running the camp, and Abigail had spent the past several months working on a similar transition. That of helping Josie quit her job and scale back operations at Shepherd's Creek to make things more manageable for the family. It was no longer about Uncle Joe and his vision, or even Abigail's interpretation of how things needed to work for the family, but everyone doing what was best for the family and the stables and making those decisions together.

Which gave Abigail the ability to move

to Camp Guffey and to help Isaac live his dream of helping the foster kids there.

An errant wave crashed over them, splashing Abigail higher on her legs, causing her to jump. Isaac's arms came around her tightly as he held her closely to him.

"Careful," he said, kissing her on top of the head.

Abigail smiled. "I don't mind. I love this experience, and I love sharing it with you."

As she stepped out of his arms, she said, "So, what is this about the horses? I didn't see that in the plans for Camp Guffey."

Isaac looked thoughtful for a moment, then shrugged. "It never was, but I keep thinking of how you've given up so much for me. I know you love it at Camp Guffey, and you're making it your home, but it doesn't seem right for you to have a home without horses."

Truthfully, as much as she loved being at Camp Guffey and discovering all the activities to be done there, she did miss her horses. But they'd been so busy with everything else that she hadn't had time to give it much thought or consider how they could change things.

But obviously, her husband had noticed. And planned for her, knowing what horses meant to her. Which was one of the things she loved about Isaac. All this time, he saw her, and he looked for ways to meet her needs, even when she hadn't noticed them for herself.

Isaac had once asked her who took care of her, and she'd proudly said that she took care of herself. Now, she could say that Isaac took care of her, far better than she ever did.

"I would love horses," Abigail said. "But I'm going to need your help."

Isaac nodded. "I know. But I also know that together, we can do anything."

He pulled her close and kissed her gently, then released her.

"Besides, I miss Simba. And I know it's not good for a horse to be alone, so we need to find him a friend. Even if we don't have horses for the campers, it would be nice to go on rides with you."

Abigail wrapped her arms around him and kissed him again. "That sounds wonderful. You've made all my dreams come true, even the ones I didn't know I had."

Isaac took her hand. "And that's just the beginning."

* * * * *

*If you enjoyed this Shepherd's Creek book,
be sure to read the previous books in
Danica Favorite's miniseries:*

**Journey to Forgiveness
The Bronc Rider's Twins**

Available now from Love Inspired!

Dear Reader,

It's so funny how my life always mimics something I'm writing about, even though I never plan it. But God likes to use things in our lives, and this was no different. Sometimes I feel a lot like Abigail because I spend so much time taking care of others that I can't always see what I need. But also, I feel like Isaac at times, facing fears because I know it's what I need to do to move forward in my life. To tell the truth, there's a bit of me in every character, and I suspect, a bit of them in us all.

No matter where you feel like you fit with my characters, I hope you know that God sees you. He loves you, no matter what.

Also, for my daughter, Simba is the best horse ever. That is all.

Be sure to follow me on social media through my website at DanicaFavorite.com.

Blessings to you and yours,
Danica Favorite

Get 3 FREE REWARDS!

We'll send you 2 FREE Books plus a FREE Mystery Gift.